BLOOD ON THE LAND

The smell hit me first, the stench of burning meat. One of the cows had not gotten away when the prairie scavengers fired the lean-to, and the smell of charring beef mingled with the acrid smell of burning hide. I screamed and ran toward the house.

My pa lay by the well, rifle clutched in his hands. His face was turned away from me, but the blood clotted on the back of his head. I found my mother in the doorway. I saw the bloodstains across her dress and knew I'd never hear her voice again.

I stared up at the sky and cried out my pain and fear.

KANSAS BLOOD

BY JAY MITCHELL

ZEBRA BOOKS
KENSINGTON PUBLISHING CORP.

ZEBRA BOOKS

are published by

Kensington Publishing Corp.
475 Park Avenue South
New York, NY 10016

First printing: February 1986

Printed in the United States of America

Prologue

The scream shattered the fine Kansas morning.

At first the sound was so foreign I couldn't put a name to it, but the gunshot cracked right after the cry and it abruptly became quite real. Suddenly I was on my feet, running barefoot across the grassy plain. The wildflowers I'd picked tumbled down my dress, unheeded.

I hardly felt the snagging prairie weeds catching at my dress or the sharp stones biting into my feet. The ground, uneven and rough, made my view of the horizon jumbled. My stumbling movements merged blue sky into the grasslands of the High Plains, hindering my flight.

Already I was out of breath, gasping in the warm air, but guilt and fear kept me running. Fear because of trouble at the farmhouse. Guilt because I had wandered much too far.

I heard more gunshots as I pelted over the plains, sickened by the sound. It wasn't my pa's rifle I heard, or the pistol he kept by his bedside. Strangers. Somehow strangers had come to the farmhouse, and with them came trouble.

By now my sobs had freed themselves from my chest, breaking up my labored breathing. I ignored the constriction, ignored the icy-cold, roiled sensation in my belly, and ran.

As I stumbled up the hill by the cornfield I saw the first billows of smoke rising on the air. Somehow I dragged in another choking breath and kept going, nearly tumbling headfirst down the hill.

Faintly I heard the ringing bark of a hound, the blue tick we called Tracker. If there were trouble he'd do what he could to stall it, but against guns a dog was easy prey. I feared for the hound, but I feared more for my family. All I could think to do was *run*, run to Pa, a big enough man able to stop nearly any brewing trouble.

Cottonwoods lined the river behind the house, but a few of the big trees crept up toward the prairie plains as if to escape the regimental lines of the others. I had no thought for the big one on my right as I topped the rise and hurried down, but I guess the tree had an eye out for me. My foot caught a root and I fell hard, banging my jaw into the ground hard enough to shoot stars in my head and make it spin. My eyes crossed and I bit my bottom lip, bringing blood salty and quick. It hurt so bad I just lay there with a mouthful of grit, trying to suck in some air.

That was how I missed being murdered by prairie scavengers who killed my family and rode away while I lay sprawled in the dust, fighting tears of pain and frustration, and fear.

PART I

"Toby"

Chapter One

I'd grown up fast in the two years since the murder of my family. I'd had to as a matter of survival. And I guess somewhere along the line I grew up changed, because no more was I the good-natured, light-minded fifteen-year-old girl my folks had brought with them from Ohio to the High Plains of Kansas.

Death and tragedy dogged the heels of other emigrants in the 1880s and though the names were different, the stories always seemed the same. For me a large part of my life ended that spring morning, but the bigger part was beginning.

The morning that changed my life even more started quietly enough. I felt dirty and wanted a bath badly, so once my chores were done and I'd had some breakfast, I gathered up clean clothes, soap and a rough towel. With the rifle tucked into the crook of my arm I headed to the river.

Patch, the tomcat, cavorted in the warmth of the spring air. He was an ugly, gray cat with a yellowish patch across one side of his head and an ear. Pa had picked him up in town as a tiny kitten. The bluetick who also trailed me had followed our wagon faithfully all the way from Ohio. I was glad to have Tracker with me now. A good dog, I often thought contentedly to myself, was worth any man. As long as I had my animals I wasn't in total solitude, though close to it. I preferred it that way. Critters had more smarts than most people, and made better company.

Tracker went off in pursuit of something more interesting than my bath, and the cat chased after a butterfly. I stripped out of my faded, too-small dress at the edge of a pool and dove in, glad to shed both clothes and dirt.

The bath was wonderful and I regretfully climbed out after spending a long time submerged. I dressed in a clean dress as faded as the other, smoothed the threadbare wrinkles and gathered up my gear. I headed back up the hill.

I'd gone no farther than twenty feet when a sound and movement in thick grasses halted me cold. I dropped my things and swung my rifle into firing position, squinting down the sights.

"You'd best sing out before I shoot!" I called fiercely.

I guess I didn't sound too fierce at that; I could hear the quaver in my voice. It made me angry to show my fear like that. Fear never threatened anybody.

The grass moved before I could try again, and this time a voice accompanied it. "Please—don't shoot. . . ."

"What do you want?"

"Help—I need your help. That's all."

"You hurt?"

"Shot."

Shot, is he, I considered as I chewed my bottom lip.

I didn't particularly want trouble of any sort coming onto my land, let alone shooting trouble. But if he was hurt badly I didn't want him dying on me here. So I started to skirt around him, approaching cautiously.

"Keep in mind I got a rifle on you," I warned. He was close enough for me to hear the laughter in his answer. "I don't think I have the strength for it. You're safe enough—from me."

When I got up to him I saw he wasn't going to cause me any trouble. He was hurt too badly for it. He lay on his belly, one arm outstretched like he'd been using it to pull himself along. The other one he held close to his left side. His shirt was dirty and torn, and dark bloodstains spread across his left shoulder. I saw newer, redder stains wetting the fabric as well.

"No strength," I muttered softly. "I can see that clear enough. You look about done in."

"I am," he said softly.

I withdrew a step, startled by his voice, for I'd thought he'd fainted from the pain. His face was white and gaunt like he'd been doing some activity far past his physical ability, and the pain painted blue shadows under his eyes.

"You've got to help me," he whispered. "I can't run anymore."

His eyes opened and I stared down at him, rifle still clenched in my hands. I saw his eyes wander dazedly up my bare legs, over my faded green dress and then to my face. I saw disappointment in his face.

"Just a girl," he murmured. He swallowed heavily, keeping his eyes open with effort. "Fetch your pa, would you? I—I need help."

11

"If you need it, you'll get it from me," I said brusquely. "*If* you truly need it."

The free hand stretched and dug fingers into the grass, tautening to pull himself upright. His teeth shone in a fearful rictus of concentration, and the strain in his face drove away my suspicions.

"Don't," I said, kneeling to set the rifle aside. "Don't spend any more strength than you have to. I'll—I'll tend to it. Stay still."

I put my fingers to the hole in his shirt as he subsided into silence, breathing hard from exertion. He wasn't lying. The bullet hole in his shoulder reminded me forcibly what I'd found in my family. The sight brought the whole recollection back as if it were two days old rather than two years, and I swallowed heavily.

"Listen," I said to him, "I can't move you by myself. You'll have to help me. The house ain't far. At least if you're bound to die you'll do it in a decent bed, what's due a man, not lying in the dirt."

Black lashes fluttered as his eyes came open. "I've never heard someone encourage me in quite that manner."

I stared at him, then shrugged. "Come on, stranger. Let's get this done with."

He mumbled something and raised himself, screwing up his face at the pain. I moved in and lent a hand, then together we somehow struggled to our feet.

"You're heavy!" I gasped, trying to remain upright.

"Sorry," he mumbled, weaving on his feet as he tried a step.

He was about to keel over, but I hung on like a dog with a bone. I pulled his right arm over my shoulders and let him lean on me, though I staggered under his weight. He wasn't much help, but he tried.

"Come on," I gasped through clenched teeth. "Walk. Slow and easy. The house ain't far ahead. Use me to hold some of your weight."

"You're the best crutch a man could ever have," he said softly, and I grunted in response.

I discovered what was meant by dead weight. The burden I supported wasn't quite dead—yet—but close to it. He was wobbly and stumbling, but I could feel him tense up with the effort to do it on his own. He never complained, though it must have hurt something fierce. Maybe he couldn't force anything out between his clenched teeth.

"Don't think about it," I ordered. "Just walk."

"I *am* walking."

"Lean on me some more if you need to."

"If I do, you'll collapse."

"Let me worry about that."

"Willingly."

When we got to the house I used a foot to shove open the door of the bedroom my parents had used. For a moment I felt a wavering regret, for I hadn't been in the room since, but had no time to think about putting him somewhere else. He was due a good bed and time to himself for healing.

"Here's the bed," I said.

"I never thought I'd see one of these again," he gasped, and fell forward onto it.

I winced as he landed, but it didn't seem to bother him. I put a hand on his good arm.

"Here, let me help you turn over."

He muttered something and shifted, pushing himself onto his side. I halted, stricken by something in his face.

"They want me dead," he murmured, nearly incoherent with pain and weakness. "Dead . . ."

"Who does?" I demanded harshly, stiffening. His blue eyes were wide, staring, but saw no more than his own images. "They *shot* me."

"*Who?*" I hissed sharply, but saw I'd get no answer. He'd passed out.

The bullet had gone through his left shoulder, leaving a clean hole with no ragged edges. But he'd lost a lot of blood, and dragging himself along the ground had put dirt in the wound, causing inflammation. I made a poultice after cleaning the wound thoroughly, and bandaged the wound carefully.

A low growl came through the door as I finished and it climbed in pitch as Tracker scrabbled into the house, toenails scratching deeply into the wood floor. He came through the door as fast as he could move on the slick wood, sliding, lips drawn back in a menacing snarl.

I put a hand out to him. "Tracker! No! It's safe, *safe*. Settle down, old hound, settle down."

My tone eased the dog and he quieted his loud growl, but I could still hear the low rumble in his throat as he posted himself at the end of the bed. He was hackled from shoulders to tail, tensed to leap onto the stranger if I asked for it.

I hushed the dog again and he finally retreated to a corner by the door, curling down in the floor, keeping a wary eye on the man in the bed. I felt safe now, even if the stranger did mean me harm. I trusted Tracker to take down any man in an instant.

I cut my patient free of the bloodied shirt and dropped it so the hound could smell it, accustoming himself to the stranger's scent. He'd still jump him if I ordered, but I'd have no battle if it wasn't necessary. I left his pants alone; a man is due his dignity even while hurt. I pulled up a chair and sat with him, fearing he might grow fevered. I used the time to study on what sort of a man he was, or might be.

He didn't look a whole lot older than me. The sick white color of his face made him take after a child, I thought, seeking peace in the big bed. His hair was dark and shaggy, needing cutting.

A man's character shows in his face, so I studied his closely to get an idea of him, vulnerable in sleep. His jaw was firm and sharp, as if he could be stubborn. The bones of his face were clear and good. His was a young face, but I thought the age might be coming very soon. Out here a man grew up fast.

His eyes, though closed now in sleep, were deep blue and fringed with black lashes long enough to do any girl proud. But there was no hint of girlishness in him.

I sat on my chair and stared into his face, wondering apprehensively what had brought him practically to my doorstep, shot and running, badly frightened, yet wearing no gunbelt.

"Who are you?" I asked softly. "Who are you, stranger, and why have you come?"

He lay quietly in the bed, telling me nothing as he slept and dreamed and began to heal. Half of me badly wanted him to waken and tell me his reasons for being here; the other half refused to consider his problems. I'd learned to say little of my concerns to the townsfolk, and I knew it would be hard for me to demand explanations from him. When a person's reluctant to say anything of himself, he's equally reluctant to ask it of someone else.

I glanced around the bedroom, reflecting that I hadn't been in it since my first day back on the farm after the shootings. I had unpacked everything the bank's people had packed up, thinking I'd willingly sell and leave, and had carefully brought order back to the room my parents had made part of a home.

The lovely handworked cradle sat in a corner, dusty from lack of attention, empty of the infant who had been my brother. I felt familiar anguish squeeze my heart, then banished it as I always did. It didn't serve me to recall the pain of the first weeks I spent alone on the farm, determined to make it my own with help from no one.

I'd managed, and that was all that needed to be said.

At first, of course, I'd wished the scavengers had killed me as well. But the knowledge of whose daughter I was and a sense of family pride kept me from giving in to the pressure the townsfolk heaped on me. They claimed it wasn't possible for a lone girl to work a farm and make a decent living, but I knew better.

It was more than just stubborn pride that kept me going, more than a simple wish to prove them wrong. I felt a kinship with the land, something my pa had spoken of with warmth and wonder in his voice. The land wouldn't kill me if I respected it and

16

treated it as an equal, and gave into it when necessary. Somehow the silent land and I had struck a bargain. I never expected an easy life, so the troubles didn't bother me. I just kept on, willing to compromise with the prairie plains. They were my home.

I blew out a breath as I studied the stranger, wishing I knew exactly what he was. Over the two years alone I'd learned to fend for myself, backed by Tracker and the rifle, but my confidence didn't extend to dealing with a man who brought violence along with him. Until he roused enough to explain matters fully, I'd have to treat him with care. No telling what sort of a man he was.

"You're hurt, just like any critter," I said softly. "I won't have your death on my soul, unless God prefers to put you to some angelical task in heaven. Guess I'm stuck with you for now." I sighed. "Just don't bring your troubles to me."

Later, as I boiled a hot stew in hopes of feeding him, Tracker's growl snapped me to attention. I left the stew simmering on the stove and went to see what sort of mischief my visitor was concocting.

He was attempting to sit up, but the exercise was a failure. The sick pallor of his face had flushed with feverish color and his eyes were dazed and bright. I placed my hands on his shoulders and gently pushed him back against the pillows, glad when his small strength gave in. I smoothed the blankets over his chest and felt the trembling sickness in his bones, realizing I'd most likely miss my sleep. He'd need tending.

"Just lie easy, the rest will do you good. There's nothing more for you to run from now. Rest."

He stared wide-eyed at me. "Am I sick?"

"Can't you tell?"

He shivered and slid further beneath the covers, disoriented. "I don't feel well. I must be sick."

"You're sick, but not enough to fret over. It'll pass, and you'll feel fine again." I tried to make my face look friendly. "Do you feel like eating something?"

"No," he said plaintively, pushing his right hand through his hair. "No, I'm not hungry."

I nodded. "You will be soon enough. Well, the broth will wait. Go back to sleep."

"Are they out there?" he demanded suddenly.

"Are *who* out there?"

He shoved the trembling hand through his hair again, sucking in a deep breath. "They're there," he muttered at me. "Somewhere. They're there."

I gritted my teeth. "You've already got me sounding like an owl, asking 'who?' all the time. Do you plan on telling me?"

"Maybe I got away," he whispered blankly. "Maybe they'll forget about me."

"Let's hope so," I agreed. "Though I admit you've got my curiosity riled. Maybe if they came looking for you I'd discover what it is you're mumbling about."

His stare was oddly piercing. "Tell me they've gone. Tell me!"

I swallowed, nodding. "They're gone. Whoever they are—they're gone."

18

His color ebbed to corpse-white again. "Are you sure?"

He needed to be told. So I did. "The men who are chasing you are gone," I said flatly. "Gone. Now go to sleep."

He let his breath out in sudden relief and with it went his strength. Once more he lay deeply gone in sleep, or unconsciousness. I shivered once in response to his fear and obsessive need for safety, and left him alone.

I went to my garden and lost myself in the weeding, liking the chore as I dug in the cool, loose soil. I was always happy and content with life when I got back to the land; it did me good to work with growing things. The blue of the sky was heavy enough to blind a person, and bright sunlight lay like a blanket across the land. I forgot my sick stranger as I tended the vegetables, and felt the tenseness leave my body as I worked.

I grew thirsty and headed for the well. Tracker interrupted my drink of cool water with a bark of alarm, and I dropped the dipper and ran.

He was sitting upright again and this time he'd accomplished it. I stopped dead in the bedroom doorway, wondering just how strong a man could be in fever. I doubted I could force him back down if he didn't feel like doing it.

Tracker stood stiff-legged, growling and hackled. I put a hand to his neck as he moved to my left side. He would attack only if I gave the word, or if the man threatened me. I held my tongue, wondering.

He glanced wildly around the room in a mixture

19

of fear and aggression. Fresh blood stained the bandages and I realized in irritation he'd broken open his wound again. My hands went to my hips.

"Lie back down, mister. You'll do yourself no good thrashing around like that, and you're only making more work for me to look after you. Lie back down, or I'll put the dog on you."

Maybe my words had some effect or maybe his strength gave out right then, but he did slump back on the pillows. I smiled to myself as he stared at the snarling hound. Then he wrenched his gaze to me.

"Who are you?"

"My name is Lonnie Ryan. I'm the one who nearly stumbled across you by the river earlier. You always creep up on a person like that?"

He blinked at my tone, though he continued to stare at me, a blank look in his eyes. He looked thoughtfully at me without the wild-eyed glare of before.

"Then I really am here."

"Of course you're here," I said. "Where else would you be?"

"I thought—I thought maybe I'd dreamed it all."

I lifted an eyebrow suspiciously. "All? Or just the part where I found you?"

He swallowed. "I really did get away."

I sighed. "I sure hope you make better sense when you're awake and alert. So far this passle of trouble you're involved in sounds like some sort of a lunatic's tale."

Color left his face. "I can't tell you. I don't know you."

I bit at a finger reflectively, trying to piece together

whatever it was I'd gotten myself mixed up in. He didn't look crazy to me, just sick and scared, and apprehensive about what my intentions were. Well, we were even on that. I removed my finger and smiled soothingly at him.

"If I'm all you have to worry about, it ain't much. You may as well sleep peacefully. I don't shoot without just cause."

"Shoot?" he asked warily.

"Of course someone already beat me to it," I said lightly.

His brows lowered into a frown. "What are you talking about?"

"I haven't figured that out yet. But you weren't making any sense either, so I thought I might try it." I sighed wearily. "You are safe here, you know, for the time being. So long as you make no threat to me."

"To you? Why would I?"

I shrugged. "I guess that's your secret. In addition to the one you've already got."

The puzzled look faded and he was withdrawn once more. "I can't tell you."

"Fine," I said. "Can I at least replace the poultice? Turn on your side."

He did as I asked and never said a word as I fixed a new poultice and wrappings for his shoulder. Already some of the swelling had gone down, though the inflammation still looked angry and sore. The fever was fading for now, but I knew he'd sicken again come nighttime.

"Where's everyone else?" he asked once I'd finished.

"I'm all there is."

21

He stared at me. "All?"

"All," I said firmly. "I'm alone out here, but don't go thinking I'm helpless. I was never that."

"But you must have people here. A family."

"None."

Perhaps something in my tone sounded guarded, for he hesitated as he spoke again. "What happened? Indians?"

"Why do folks always lay trouble at the doorstep of Indians?" I asked bitterly. "What happened to me came at the bloody hands of white men."

"White men!"

"Plains scavengers."

"I'd sooner call them animals," he said.

I shook my head. *"I'd* sooner call them men. Animals don't kill needlessly."

He opened his mouth to say something more, but I left him with his words to rid myself of the dirtied bandages. When I returned he was plucking at the bedcovers. He looked up at me curiously as I observed him silently from the doorway.

"I guess I should tell you my name."

I shrugged. "If you want to tell it."

He smiled crookedly. "So you think I'm running from the law and hiding my true identity."

"I never said that."

"I see it in your face."

"You see nothing of the sort in my face," I retorted. "Besides, you don't look the outlaw kind to me."

His eyes slid away from mine. "You might be surprised about that."

I opened my mouth to speak but he shook his head. "You're right. I'm no outlaw. I'm Tobias

Markham. Toby."

"You hungry yet, Toby Markham?"

"Some."

"I'll get you some broth."

He fed himself after I settled his pillows higher. Tracker, after a word from me, accepted that the stranger would be moving around some now. But he remained in the corner close by, watching.

Patch appeared suddenly, stalking through the bedroom door with tail held high and curled at the tip. He rambled on at great length about something in his quiet purring yowl. He landed on the bed and began kneading, so I moved in to pick him up. Toby stopped me.

"Let him stay. I don't mind."

"A cat's got no place on a sickbed."

"I'm not sick." He seemed to quail beneath my glance. "At least—I'm feeling better. Let him stay."

I cocked my head at him. "Maybe right now you feel better, but come nighttime you'll be sick as before. Fevers always worsen at night, and you had enough dirt in that wound to kill you flat out from infection alone."

He stared at Patch curling on the bed, but I could tell he wasn't seeing the cat. He was past that, somewhere far beyond. For a moment I feared he was getting feverish already, then he looked straight at me. His mouth twisted.

"I should tell you why I'm like this. Why you found me where you did."

"You should," I agreed. "But it's no business of mine. So long as you don't bring your trouble to my door, I'll leave you be about your circumstances." I held his startled stare with my own. "Out here you won't find folk as open about some things. Specially trouble. But you've been muttering about people trying to kill you, so you could say I'm a mite curious."

He swallowed and avoided my eyes. "Men," he said. "They were men. That's all."

It wasn't in me to pry, so I let it alone. But it was only fair to say I was somewhat worried about this stranger's trouble.

"Your clothes were stained and torn and the bullet wound is at least a day or two old, untended," I told him quietly. "You've got no gunbelt. Keep your silence, if you like, but don't think it ain't obvious you're running from someone."

"Isn't," he corrected absently, then stared at me as I gaped at him. "It's as plain as that, then."

"To me, and to others around these parts. We don't talk much. We don't particularly feel the need."

His eyes had gone hard and bright and his voice took on a mocking tone I'd heard others use to me before. "Why don't you feel the need? Aren't you sociable?"

"Sociable's got nothing to do with it! In this part of the country a man doesn't ask another man his trade unless he's willing to tell it, and he'll speak first if he is. That goes for personal things, too."

He was amused at my expense. "But you're no man, Lonnie Ryan, and there's a lot about you that puzzles me."

My head came up, scenting something familiar. I'd heard this said many times before by townsfolk

24

despairing of my future.

I took myself and the empty bowl to the door. My injured guest stared after me, waiting for a word in return.

I shrugged and grinned lopsidedly at him. "Stay puzzled."

Chapter Two

When I went in to check him later he heard me coming and hurriedly shoved himself up on an elbow. I saw the twinge of pain cut across his face as he fell back on his bad shoulder, but the stubborn look in his eyes kept me from chiding him for it. I waited, and he finally settled himself against the pillows.

"Lonnie, I'm sorry if I made you mad by what I said earlier. I didn't mean it."

His big, dark-rimmed eyes were on my face, and the pallor of his sickness softened my tone. "Of course you meant it. Save your apologies; I'd rather you'd say what you think flat out, instead of making me pick and choose the real meaning."

He still seemed embarrassed. "Well, maybe so, but I'm sorry I said it the way I did. I should be beholden to you for what you're doing."

"Don't let that stop you from saying what you think. And I'm not doing anything special. I'd do the same for a hurt critter."

His eyes narrowed. "Sounds like you've got more respect for animals than for people."

I folded my arms. "I do. I've lived with both, and I'll take a creature of the wild over a man any day."

"So why bother with me? Why not just leave me where you found me?"

"Where the law can find you?" I asked, grinning at his discomfiture. "Anyway, you'd die. I may not think too highly of folks in general, but nothing says I should turn my back on a hurt man. So I decided you could stay here till you're better. You'll be on your way soon enough."

"As soon as you've got me back on my feet?" he asked, mocking again.

I studied him, eyes narrowed. "Maybe sooner. I could always haul you into town in the buckboard and dump you. Then you'd be out of my way."

"There's a town close by?" he asked sharply.

"Ridgely. It's twelve miles, give or take a foot."

"I could go there." He sounded absent and thoughtful. "More people mean more safety."

"I'll not kick you out before you're healed," I told him. "But I'll take you there when you're fit."

Suddenly he smiled, all charm and bright looks as his blue eyes lit up and his teeth showed. The smile chased away the sick look of him.

I narrowed my eyes at him thoughtfully. Any man with a hint of charm is dangerous. If I'd thought Toby Markham was one of the breed, I'd have left him at the river.

"I'll go when it suits me," he said lightly.

"You'll go when I say you're fit."

He shook his head, still smiling and bright-eyed. "No, Lonnie. I'll choose my own way. I always do."

He sounded light and carefree with no worries at

all. Something about his manner made me hackle up like Tracker and I longed to take some of the spunk out of him.

"I reckon that's what accounted for the bullet in your shoulder, then."

It sobered him. The bright look faded and the smile went with it. He recalled where he was, and why.

"I *am* beholden to you for this, Lonnie."

"Don't keep it on your mind. Your kind remembers to be beholden only when it suits."

He looked stubborn. I'd been right about the jaw. "Don't make up your mind about me too soon. I might not be the man you think I am."

I matched my smile to his. "Don't count yourself so all-fired important to me, stranger. I don't think much of you one way or another."

He took it as a challenge. "What if I was rich? You'd pay me mind then."

I counted that for what it was—all bluster with nothing behind it. Something to rattle me where I stood, wearing faded, threadbare clothes and no shoes. To him, wealth would be something to threaten with, something to make a person without feel small. To me, it represented something I didn't need.

My smile went lopsided. "I *could* say that if you were rich you'd not be in this fix. But I won't."

He tried to play my way. "But what if I said I'd been bushwhacked for money and left for dead?"

I considered that. He *had* been shot and possibly left for dead, as he said. But I wouldn't give in that easily.

"What do you count as riches?"

"Riches?" He stared at me, then laughed. "Money, of course. Gold. Or the means to make money."

I laughed outright at him. "You're too simple, like the rest. A fortune-chaser after gold."

He frowned at my tone. "No, not gold. Not me. At least not yet. I'll leave that for later. I have plans for something else." Suddenly he looked lost, and his voice showed it. "At least—I *had* plans."

"Getting shot changed them, huh?"

He looked sour. "For now."

I tried to be kind. "You're not the first to chase after the pot at the end of the rainbow. Gold fever is a real sickness."

"I wasn't after gold! I told you that."

I shrugged. "so you've tacked your dreams on something else. Again, you're not the first. What is it, cattle? Homesteading?"

"Buffalo," he muttered.

I stared at him. *"Buffalo!"*

He sounded defensive. "I wanted to be a buffalo hunter. I wanted to become one of the men who went out and shot the shaggy beasts. I wanted to be the best. I still might do it."

I found the chair and dropped into it, grinning delightedly to myself. Suddenly he sounded like a little boy with big dreams, dreams that glittered dancingly. But only dreams. I laughed a little. Buffalo.

"They're a smelly bunch," I told him. "There's not many left. Too many hunters before you left them to rot, not using much but maybe the tongue and the brisket and the hide. The Indians had more

29

use for them. Yet you want to kill off some more." I shook my head. "You don't know a thing about being rich."

"What's that got to do with buffalo?"

"Being rich," I told him from my heart, "has more to do with it than just money or gold. Have you never heard about the riches of the land?"

He sounded bitter, and looked it. "Do you mean to lecture me on what it's like to break your back on a farm? If so, don't bother. I know what it is to farm. My folks have a place in Minnesota."

"And you—farm-bred—have no respect for the land and what it brings?"

He shook his tousled head. "I know what it brings. Heartache and hard work, drought and flooding rains. It makes a man old before his time." He shifted his eyes from a spot on the bed to me. "And a woman old before *her* time."

He meant it to hurt. For a moment it nearly did, then I dismissed it as I had for so long. I knew well enough what the life meant. Maybe at the beginning I hadn't been intended to wind up alone and hard-pressed to live, but I was still willing to accept what happened. Toby Markham's biting tone only made me all the more firm in my convictions.

"You're a fool," I told him softly. "I know the land can bring all those things, if you fight it. But if you work *with* it, learn to live with what it brings, you can make yourself rich. As rich as any man with money jingling in his pockets."

"You delude yourself, Lonnie. Wealth is measured in sections of land, or the size of your house, or how many head of cattle you run. Even the kind of clothes you wear."

"Your clothes ain't so almighty fancy for a man who places wealth in what he wears."

His jaw got the stubborn set again. "That's because something I had no control over happened. I never got a fair chance to start earning my fortune."

"I'll go along with that," I agreed. "A bullet happened." I sighed and shook my head. "I don't understand why so many people come out here looking for a stake. Usually it's gold. My family found wealth in the land this house stands on, and the forty acres along with it. We counted ourselves rich enough with all this."

"Tell that to your dead folks, buried in this land you love so much," he said sharply.

Heat flooded my face as pain and rage fought for dominance in my soul. My hands balled into fists so hard my palms hurt, and I clenched my teeth. Slowly I rose from the chair and stood over him, glaring down at him.

"You keep talking like that and you *will* get yourself left where I found you!"

"Lonnie—wait! Lonnie . . ."

I whipped around as I reached the door, conscious of Tracker's growl coming from the corner. The dog was up and hackled, bothered by the tone of my voice. For an angry moment I was tempted to let him at Toby, but the fury faded as quickly as it had come. I took a deep breath and saw his swallow.

"Lonnie—please. I must apologize again. I had no call to say that."

31

"You'd best not say it again." I turned and left the room, and the man in it.

He thrashed that night and I didn't get much sleep as I sat by his side, nursing him through the dark. As I'd expected, the fever had come up again, burning his flesh, and I did what I could to ease his discomfort with cool, damp cloths. I wet down his burning forehead and chest, and waited for the fever to break.

He talked a little, but mostly it was a string of mumbles that made no sense. I listened closely to the clearest words, trying to piece together the trouble on his mind, wondering how serious it might be. Also I was concerned for him; a body only heals clean if the mind is at rest, and his wasn't.

He mumbled something about buffalo, and I smiled. Strange notions brought people to the High Plains of Kansas and the California goldfields, and his notion to hunt buffalo wasn't new to anybody save himself. But if he was really fleeing a farming life in Minnesota, I figured the life of a buffalo runner did sound pretty exciting. So long as you didn't know what the life really was.

I'd heard enough, naturally, and had seen my share of buffalo runners passing through town, and I wasn't impressed by the smelly, close-keeping men. But I guess that was only fair. The daily toil of my life likely didn't spark much interest in anyone else. It certainly hadn't for my unwanted guest.

I heard more snatches of talk out of him, and this time I didn't smile. He talked of shooting and murder, and guilt. I froze on my chair, hands clenched together as I heard the damning words. Was he only the naive farmer-boy he claimed? Or was he something else, something dangerous?

"Toby Markham," I said softly into the flickering lantern light. "Toby Markham, you'd best heal fast. Someone put a bullet through your shoulder, and likely meant it to kill. What have you done?"

By morning the fever faded and his troubled sleeping eased. I was tired myself from sitting up all night, and dragged myself out of the chair with effort. I went out and reheated the broth, figuring he'd be hungry again by now.

He was awake when I returned to his bedside. I saw quick fear in his eyes and halted abruptly, startled by the look on his face. Then he saw me clearly, and the expression went away. He stared at me in confusion as I came closer and held out the bowl and spoon.

"Morning, Toby."

He pulled himself together after a moment and shoved himself up in the bed, against the pillows, reaching for the bowl. He spooned it into his mouth and ate like a starving man with no care for taste or temperature. I counted it a good sign.

Over the bowl his eyes watched me like a wary animal. I waited silently and took it from him as he finished the broth. My silence seemed to calm him at last, for he smiled at me as I turned to leave.

"Will you come sit with me?"

"Maybe later. I've got chores to do."

He dropped his eyes from mine and picked at the quilt. I waited silently in the doorway, patient. He was sorting something out in his head. Finally he seemed to make a decision, and lifted his steady gaze to mine once more.

"Lonnie, I was pushing for a fight yesterday."

"Were you, now." I studied him expressionlessly. "Why's that, Mister Markham?"

He sighed. "I'm —I'm not always like that. It was rude, pushing you to see what you'd say. My mother would be ashamed."

I nearly laughed, but kept it from him. "So you don't really want to be a buffalo runner."

He shifted against the pillows, wincing in pain. "No, I spoke the truth about that. I did come out here to hunt buffalo. But what I said about being rich didn't need saying. At least the way I said it." He looked straight at me. "And what I said about your family was wrong."

"You already apologized for that."

"I know, but I didn't do it very well." He rubbed at his forehead. "Sometimes—sometimes I talk too much about things I don't think enough about. My father was always taking the back of his hand to me for that. I guess I just wanted to see what you'd do."

"You saw."

His grin came, quick as lightening and just as bright. "I saw. You fought back."

"I'm a good one for that, so long as I feel it's called for."

He laughed, then the gaiety left his face. He was suddenly serious. Changeable as quicksilver, this man was.

"Come back, Lonnie, when you're done with chores. I'd like to talk to you."

"Why?"

He shrugged his good shoulder. "Just to talk. For

34

company's sake. Is that so strange?"

"It is to me." I sighed and nodded. "All right, I'll come back. When I'm done."

I left him and headed out to do the morning chores. It meant collecting eggs from the henhouse, milking Princess the cow, and forking fodder to both the cow and the brown mare. Princess was due to drop her calf in a couple of weeks, so I was extra careful about what she ate. I wanted a little heifer so I'd have two milkers. If she dropped a bull-calf I'd sell it to the farmer who owned the bull I'd bred Princess to.

I'd feed myself once the chores were done. I meant to have bacon and cool, fresh milk along with fried eggs. I ate big for a girl, but it never stayed on me. I was thin as a rail and angular to boot. All burn and bone, my pa said once, tugging gently on my braid.

I favored my ma with blue eyes and dusty-blond hair, but on me her fair skin was burned brown. My nose peeled from the constant sun, staying a patchy pink like the ridged scar curving on my jaw. It was my keepsake of the fall I'd taken over the cottonwood root. The fall that had kept me from dying with the rest of my family.

Tracker came with me as I did the chores, of course, a habit he'd taken to after the murders. He rarely left me alone when I was outside, though occasionally something caught his attention. I was glad enough for it; the hound was good company and something I could trust.

One of the scavengers had taken a shot at the dog, but the bullet bounced off his skull and did no damage. The men left him for dead along with the others, but Tracker crawled off somewhere until he healed. When he returned to the house I was there, and he picked up his watchdog vigil as though he'd never left it. He had a big scar across the top of his sloping hound's head, so in a way we matched. We'd both survived our own sort of battle.

Tracker's barking jerked my attention from routine chores as I fed and watered the brown mare and Princess tied in the lean-to. His deep bell had the tone I recognized as trouble. Tracker was down by the springhouse near the river where I stored my meat, and the rifle was at the house.

I ran for the weapon, leaving the hound to fend off the trouble while I fetched it. But when I rounded the corner of the house I nearly stumbled in my haste to stop.

Toby stood by the door. He held the rifle like he knew exactly how to use it, and like he meant to.

Something in my face must have gotten to him, for he let the rifle fall to his side.

"Just what do you have in mind?" I asked rigidly, still aware of Tracker's barks echoing from the river.

"Nothing at all," he said. "I heard the barks."

I swallowed and put out a hand. "I'll take it. It's my rifle."

"Lonnie—"

"Give it to me. Now."

Wordlessly, he handed it over. I checked to make certain it was loaded, though I never left it empty. It was ready. I threw a sharp look at him.

"Stay here."

"But if there's trouble—"

"Stay here!"

I left him and went to follow the hound's frenzied barking.

Tracker had found me another stranger, but there was nothing helpless or sickly about this one. He sat his dun-colored horse in the shallows of the river, still on the far side from me. I saw the rifle scabbard at his saddle and a gunbelt at his hips, but his hands were empty save for reins.

"Good day to you, miss," he called and tipped his stained, gray hat.

I hushed Tracker and lifted the rifle into a comfortably prepared position. "You lookin' for something, mister?" I asked, throwing my voice across the water.

He nodded, though it was subtle enough because of the distance. He was dark-faced, dressed like a man used to travel, and his dun horse watered like he'd gone without.

"I'm looking for a group of men who might've passed this way a few days ago. Four men, riding hard."

"What are they to you? You the law?"

The horse snorted and stomped in the water, jerking the man's hands on the reins. He kept the horse from moving farther into the river. Respecting my rifle, I thought, and maybe even the dog.

"Once I was the law," he answered. "Not now."

"Why are you after those men then?"

I thought he smiled, but couldn't be certain. "They're worth money. I'm a bounty hunter."

"Blood money!" I exclaimed involuntarily, and saw the stiffening of his shoulders.

37

"If I don't earn it, someone else will. I'd prefer it for myself, miss. Call it what you will, but I aim to get it." He paused. "Have you seen them?"

I considered him thoughtfully. If the men he sought had prices on their heads they certainly deserved no better treatment, but I'd never felt bounty hunting was an honorable occupation. Particularly when one had been a lawman originally.

I shrugged to myself. It wasn't my concern. "What are they wanted for?"

"Murdering, thieving, rustling—what more is there? I'm not after innocents, miss. These men are dangerous."

My face tightened. "I've seen no one."

"It's possible they've split up. Have you seen a pair riding together? Maybe just a lone man?"

I swallowed, thinking instantly of the circumstances I'd found Toby in. And all his mutterings. Still, something told me to let it be.

"I've seen no one."

The horse lifted its head with a violent snort and sprayed water from its nostrils. The bounty hunter gathered his reins but remained on his side of the river.

"Miss, you'd best heed my warning. Stay inside and let your pa do the chores."

Tracker must have sensed my flash of apprehension, for he growled. I hushed him softly. "Thanks," I called. "I hope you catch 'em."

"So do I." He grinned. "I could use the money." He tipped his hat again and rode off through the trees.

I hurried back to the house and found Toby

waiting inside, standing by the rocker in the front room. I lifted the rifle carefully.

"Who are you?"

"Who am I?" he echoed, puzzled.

"Answer me."

He gaped at me. "I *told* you. Toby Markham. From Minnesota." His eyes narrowed shrewdly. "You met someone, didn't you?"

"A bounty hunter."

Color ebbed from his face and the sickness flooded back. His response was so immediate I couldn't help but tighten my grasp on the gun, ready to fire. He saw the look in my eye.

"Lonnie—"

"What do you have to fear from a bounty hunter?" I asked softly. "What is it you've done to bring a man like that on your backtrail?"

"Lonnie—you don't need that gun."

"Who are you, Toby Markham? What sort of man have I given shelter to?"

"I'm no outlaw."

"So you said, but you might've lied to me. And I spoke to the man, Toby. He's hunting outlaws. Thieves, murderers and the like." I stared him down. *"Who are you?"*

"Toby Markham," he said softly. "From Minnesota."

"You're afraid," I said flatly. "I see it in your eyes."

"I'm afraid," he admitted freely. "I have reason to be. Lonnie, please put the gun away. You don't need it."

"Don't I?" I swallowed tightly. "The bounty hunter is tracking men. Four, he said, but they might

39

have split up. How do I know you're not one of them?"

He spread his hands beneath the quilt he'd pulled around his bare shoulders. He was tall, I saw, and strong, though lacking strength still. But his face was still pinched with worry and illness, and his voice sounded sorrowed.

"I'm not one of them, Lonnie. I've told you the truth. That bounty hunter, I'm afraid, is after the men who shot me."

"You spin a pretty tale."

He shook his head helplessly. "I can't convince you, maybe, but I'm not lying. *I'm* not an outlaw. *They* are."

"Who?" I asked softly.

The spirit drained out of him. "I only took your gun down to see if it was loaded. That's all. I just needed to know I was safe."

"Outlaws don't go unarmed," I said quietly, recalling his weaponless arrival.

He smiled sadly. "Not often, I'd think. But farmboys who stumble across a murder very rarely carry guns."

"A murder," I echoed.

He nodded. "I think I'd better tell you. All of it. Especially now that a bounty hunter has appeared."

I saw he had gotten shaky and nearly weaved as he stood by the rocker. I gestured. "Do it sitting down."

He nearly fell into it, sucking his breath in and wincing as he settled his bad shoulder against the chair. He was dead-white and sweat beaded against his forehead. By rights I knew he should be in bed, but he wouldn't have gotten that far.

40

I put the rifle up on its pegs by the door, knowing now he meant me no harm, and sat on the bench at the table. I folded my hands and stared at them, figuring it might make his confession easier if I didn't stare at him. His voice was quiet, but loud enough for me to hear deep feelings echoing in his tone.

He started at the beginning.

"I really am from Minnesota. My family has a dairy there. A good place, but I grew tired of the life. I just wasn't made to be a dairyman or a farmer." His eyes flicked to me. "Regardless of what you say about the riches of the land."

I smiled faintly. "Go on. Tell me your tale."

"There was no real need for me there. I've got two older brothers, both big men, like my father. Well, he always favored them. Said I took after my mother too much—with all the book learning I wanted."He smiled wryly. "She taught me what it meant to read, about the magic held in books, and I did more reading than working. Something my pa couldn't understand."

"A lot of people don't take to book learning," I told him. "I never got the chance, though I read and cipher, of course."

He smiled sadly. "I liked reading far better than tending the dairy. So my pa ran roughshod over me, expecting me to handle the heavy work like my brothers did. I couldn't, and I hated it. It made me sour on farming. That's why I cut at you so badly."

"Everyone's got his reasons."

He sighed. "Well, I read lots of stories about the West. My favorites were tales of the buffalo hunters. I

41

read about the big hunts and the men who went on them."

He sounded thoughtful, but I couldn't let him go on thinking romantic book thoughts of the buffalo runners. It would do him no good at all.

"I told you about your buffalo hunters yesterday. They're few now—the big animals—they should be left alone to grow old in peace."

"But to me it was the only place I could go, the only place I wanted to go. Far from the farm, and it sounded so exciting."

"So one day you just up and left your kin."

He shook his head. "Not so fast as that. I waited till I turned twenty—three months ago. I'd done all my thinking about what it meant should I leave, and I didn't figure my pa'd miss me that much. More trouble than I was worth, he always said. I was always a trial to him."

I couldn't keep the smile out of my voice. "Youngest sons generally are. Fathers are spoiled by the time the last one comes along."

He grunted. "Well, I took my savings—which weren't much, of course—and came out here to Kansas."

"Leaving no word?"

Toby was suddenly defensive. "Why should I leave them word? My father never wasted many on me but to say what a disappointment I was to him. So I left. It's my own life; I can spend it how I like."

I opened my mouth to protest, then shut it. This was something I couldn't figure. It went against what I'd been taught, how I'd been raised. With loving parents, of course, but strong ones who brought me up to respect their wishes, respecting my own as well. I frowned at Toby.

"So you didn't haul your own load alongside your brothers. You just wandered off when you felt like it."

The stubborn set crept into his jaw and his eyes went sharp. "That's what I call freedom, Lonnie. A man should be able to pull up his roots when it strikes him to do it, without a thought to what it means. Otherwise he's nailed his boots to the floor. That's not what I want out of life."

"No," I said. "You want money and adventure, like every other young buck hightailing it from a good home in the East."

"*You* did it. Your family came here from somewhere else."

"Ohio. But we did it together, as a family, not as a boy running off from work he didn't like."

Suddenly, shockingly, he grinned. "You're tied to the ground, girl. You've planted your roots. You've lost your freedom, while I've kept mine."

"*Your* freedom brought you a bullet."

His jaw tightened. "It's for me to choose."

I rubbed at my eyebrow. "Since you're so all-fired bent on doing it, I guess so. I don't suppose you got that bullet by doing something against the law, did you?"

He sighed heavily. "Back to that, are we? You really don't trust me."

"No. Why should I? You're just some stranger who wandered onto my land after getting himself shot."

He grunted, looking worn to the bone. I nearly said he should go back to bed, but if he felt like telling

43

me his reasons for being in his circumstances, I wouldn't stop him. I wasn't one for prying a person's history free, but I wouldn't protest much if he willingly told me.

"I didn't break the law. I value freedom too much to risk losing it to jail or a hangman's noose. I just tried to become a buffalo hunter."

"Like you'd read in books."

He rested his head against the back of the chair and closed his eyes. "Like I'd read in books. I bought a rifle and a horse, and packed some supplies. I headed out to find some hunters I could join up with. It wasn't easy."

"No, I can guess it wasn't," I agreed. "Runners are a close bunch; they don't cotton to newcomers. Particularly farmboys from Minnesota."

He began to rock the chair. Both hands hung lightly over the arms of the wooden rocker and I saw his fingers were slack in relaxation. One foot kept the rocker moving slowly, carefully, and I realized his wound must be hurting him.

"Toby, you can stop. You can tell me later."

"No," he said softly. "I'll tell it to you now. All of it."

"There's no need—"

"I'll do it." His eyes came open and focused on mine. "Will you listen?"

"I'll listen."

He sighed and went on. "A couple of hunting parties turned me down flat, hooting at me, saying they didn't need anyone and certainly didn't want a greenhorn kid tagging along. I'm a decent shot, so I kept looking for hunters, hoping I'd find a group who wasn't so particular. A month ago I found some others. I was riding in to camp to ask if I could join them." He laughed once, lightly. "I didn't really hold much hope; my dream looked pretty shabby by now. But I thought I'd ask."

"What did they say?"

"I never got to ask. Before I got too close I saw men with them who didn't look like hunters. They seemed different, somehow, dangerous. Something told me to hang back."

He stopped. There was a strange note in his voice. I couldn't really put a name to it, but I gathered something unexpected had occurred, something that had accounted for a change in carefree, careless Toby Markham.

He picked at the quilt as I watched him, lost in his recollections. By now I knew he wasn't an outlaw, as I'd feared; he was exactly what he sounded like. Someone out chasing bright, elusive dreams. People like him didn't normally carry the sort of trouble that accounted for shooting. At least, not very often.

Toby, when he continued, looked and sounded much older. I listened silently.

"The men had pistols, and they held the hunters at gunpoint. I wasn't so far away I couldn't see what happened. I dropped off my horse and left him, crawling in closer. The buffalo hunters were bunched together, unarmed, helpless. The others— the men with guns—were digging through their supplies."

A shiver ran down my spine. "Scavengers."

"What?"

"Men I told you about. Men that rob the runners

45

for supplies and gold." I swallowed. "When they're not off killing helpless settlers."

He looked puzzled. "But there were no hides, Lonnie. I thought they'd want the skins to sell themselves, but it wasn't that. I couldn't hear what was said, but one of the gunmen came up with a pouch and shouted something. He was laughing. I figured they were after money. And then . . ." He had to stop and draw a breath. He wet his lips. "Then they killed the buffalo hunters. Just shot them down without letting them speak a word."

I heard the horror and amazement in his voice. I was not hardened to violence, exactly, but I'd learned to put it away in my mind so I couldn't be bothered by it. It did me no good to worry over it. I nodded.

"That's why people are so helpless against men like that. They kill on a whim."

He sighed, still rocking. "I was afraid they'd find me too. I climbed back on my horse and rode out of there as fast as I could." He stopped rocking and stared at me. "You'd call me a coward, wouldn't you?"

I stared at him and found his eyes hard and bright, and bitter. Had my own outlook made him think me unfeeling? I shook my head.

"You'd just witnessed a gang of scavengers shoot down unarmed buffalo runners. Anybody with sense would have cleared out of there. I'd have done it."

"You?" he asked, mocking.

I met his look steadily. "Even me. Odd though it sounds, I do admit."

He gave in to my counterattack and nodded. "Well, I rode to the nearest town and told the sheriff what I'd seen."

"A lot of people would have kept it to themselves."

"I couldn't. It was cold-blooded, outright murder. I couldn't let what I'd seen weigh in my mind and do nothing about it."

"Some might've," I repeated.

"Look, I may be light-minded and careless, but I'm not that cold. I told the sheriff."

"What did he do about it?"

"Asked me to describe the men who did the shooting. So I did. He knew who they were right off."

That surprised me. "He knew who they were? From what you said?"

He nodded, gently feeling his wounded shoulder. "From the sound of it they're widely known across Kansas. It didn't take him but a minute to figure out who they were."

"Who?"

"The Barstow gang."

I sat bolt upright at the table, then spun around to face him. "Are they the men chasing you?"

His head came up and he dropped his hand away from his shoulder. His eyes were bright and curious. "You know who they are, too?"

I shoved straggly bits of hair out of my face, absently thinking I needed to redo my single braid. I wet my lips and swallowed tightly.

"Matt Barstow's gang," I said slowly. "The man that doesn't know of them is lucky for his ignorance."

"But why?"

I lifted the end of my braid to my chin and brushed at it speculatively. "It's a mean gang of men, Toby.

47

Mostly they rob banks and trains, and maybe a stage here and there, but occasionally they kill honest people if the mood strikes them." I shivered. "You're lucky you got away from the buffalo camp in one piece."

I heard growing horror in his voice. "Lonnie— they're not the ones who killed your family, are they?"

I felt sickened suddenly. It had never occurred to me before to put a name to the men who had murdered my family, but abruptly the realization struck me. The murderers were no longer nameless, faceless images. They were men.

"No one—no one knows, for certain. I didn't see it happen and no one saw any strangers around these parts. But that doesn't mean anything. It might have been the Barstows, or some other scavenging bunch of renegades."

He released a breath, sounding thoughtful. "The sheriff said the Barstows had all of Kansas afraid. I guess he wasn't just spouting off to me."

"No, not about Matt Barstow's gang. They're all that's said about them, maybe more. But it's this part of Kansas they mainly roam. Macklin County. They've got a personal reason for sticking here, I've heard."

"Which is?"

I laughed shortly, bitterly. "I only know what I hear. But I hear one of the gang is Jordy Macklin. Jacob Macklin's youngest boy."

"I don't understand."

"You sure don't know much about Kansas."

"Why should I? I haven't been here long enough to

48

learn much—other than a gang of outlaws is given free rein to roam around killing people."

I stared at him, put out by his quick words. But I held back my retort and smiled sweetly at him. "Then I'll tell you, stranger. Jacob Macklin founded this part of Kansas. He's all tied up in political things and so rich they named the county after him. He's a judge, but he's got his sights set on higher things. Like maybe governor. Anyhow, he's got a whole passle of boys and Jordy's the youngest. About your age. He turned black sheep and ran off to join up with Matt Barstow." I grinned suddenly. "Sort of what you did. Running away, I mean."

"I'm not outlaw," he growled.

"Anyway, Matt Barstow had already made his mark on the state. Him and his brother, Ben."

Toby nodded. "I know all about Ben Barstow."

"How's that? I'm the one doing all the informing."

"I," said Toby flatly, "got Ben Barstow hanged."

I was suddenly, oddly cold. My braid fell from lifeless fingers and I stared fixedly at my wounded visitor. I sought the lie in his eyes, but from the depths of them I saw only great weariness and absolute conviction. I took a careful breath.

"You got him hanged?"

"Me. Yes."

"How? How in God's green earth did you account for a thing like that?"

"It's all part of the story."

"So start talking again."

He looked at me strangely. "I thought you told me people out here don't pry into a man's past."

49

"Now I'm interested. And that was before you dragged the Barstows into this. Start talkin'."

He did. "The sheriff rounded up a posse and they went hightailing it off after the Barstows. They only caught one. Ben."

"Catching Ben is nearly as big as catching Matt himself."

"So I was told. Well, they couldn't get anywhere near the others. But they had Ben, and they put him on trial for murder."

"I thought you had to have a witness before you could put someone on trial for murder."

"They did," said Toby flatly. "They had me."

"Oh," I said faintly.

"I saw Ben Barstow shoot one of the buffalo hunters. I testified to that effect. The town was so riled up about *one* of the Barstows being caught they were ready to say Ben killed all the hunters. He didn't. Just the one. But it was enough to get him hanged."

I smiled faintly. "You must've been the town hero. Something you'd enjoy, I expect."

He flashed me a rebellious look. "I was, and I did. Then I left. My plan for hooking up with buffalo hunters had sort of lost its glitter, after all of that, so I decided to head for California." He smiled wryly. "And chase the pot of gold at the end of the rainbow."

"But something happened," I guessed. "Something—stopped you."

The smile left his face and his eyes went dark and bleak. "Matt Barstow had other ideas."

"He came after you?"

50

"Him and the rest of his gang."

I chewed at my bottom lip. "Folks say he and Ben were real close. I guess it's only natural he'd want the witness who got Ben hanged dead." I stared at him. "That's how you got shot, isn't it?"

"The Barstows caught up to me."

I was stunned. "How did you ever get away from them alive? They've *never* let anyone who could be a witness live before. You even got Ben hanged. How did you do it?"

He shifted in the rocker. "Just dumb luck. I'd been running forever, it seemed, getting weaker and weaker because of the bullet they'd put through my shoulder. Finally I just fell off my horse." He smiled in response to my incredulous expression. "I know, it isn't very romantic. But it's what happened. I rolled into some high grass and the horse kept on going. They followed him and I managed to crawl away. I nearly gave out for lack of water. I don't remember much."

"You couldn't have been far from here. You nearly made it to water. That's when I found you."

"Thank the Lord for that."

I wasn't thinking about the Lord. I had Barstows on my mind. I felt sick to my stomach, hugging myself as I stared at the floor. My voice came out harsh and strained.

"They'll be coming here. They'll come here. Looking for you—they'll come here." I swallowed. "Matt Barstow isn't stupid. He'll know you didn't die." I shivered. "Me and Ridgely will be right in their path."

"I'll leave, then, Lonnie. You'll want me to leave."

51

I looked at him and saw the bleak, lost look in his eyes. Deep down he needed help and was asking for it, but he was too proud to say it aloud. Slowly I shook my head.

"No, you'll stay here and heal. I'll not have you go before you're fit. Barstows or no."

"Don't they scare you?"

I shrugged. "I don't scare all that easy."

I think he knew. But he said nothing for a moment. "Lonnie, I'm sorry. I didn't mean for it to happen."

"Meaning things doesn't matter. It's what happens that does."

Chapter Three

Patch came in the front door and went immediately to the rocking chair. He prowled around the rocker, sniffing at Toby's legs and feet. I watched pensively as the tom chose one of Toby's big toes as a place to rub his jaw. Toby smiled down at the cat, waiting.

Patch sat down on the floor and stared up at the person in the rocker with a fixed, unwavering expression. The tip of his long tail twitched once, and without visibly tensing a hair the cat leaped. He landed lightly in Toby's lap, kneading to find a proper settling place.

Patch's ratchety purr sounded loud in the silent room, striking an odd note in the quiet left from Toby's story. The cat made me thoughtful.

Patch was never one to take to people, yet he'd picked out my visitor for attention from the outset. I wondered if there was something to the cat's actions. I knew well enough animals had the ability to sense goodness or badness in people, and I believe the creatures of the wild long before I listen to a man's lengthy stories.

There was more to Toby Markham than just his words.

"Aren't you ever going to eat breakfast?" he asked.

I focused my eyes on him. "Why?"

"Aren't you hungry?"

"What's that got to do with you?"

He was affronted. "I'm hungry, myself. I thought maybe you'd spare something for me."

"I gave you some broth earlier."

He gestured expressively. "Broth! I want something solid in my belly. Like eggs and bacon. Maybe some fried ham."

I said nothing, staring at him. He flashed the bright grin at me, bringing to light the charm I'd caught a glimpse of before. The pallor of his face and weariness in his eyes had disappeared again.

I sighed and stood up, tired of fighting him for fighting's sake. "I'll fix us both something."

Toby was right to remind me to breakfast. I found myself eating well to fill the hole in my belly, and realized I'd had no supper the night before. He ate with the appetite of a healing man over the worst. I shook my head at him.

"You must not have eaten for days."

He nodded as he scraped up the last of his eggs. "I didn't stop to take time to eat with the Barstows after me."

"No, I don't expect food came first with men like them on your trail."

I took the empty plate and fork from him and took them with mine to the sink. Then I turned and faced him sternly.

"It's time you got back to bed. You got up too soon."

"I heard the dog barking. It sounded like trouble. I just thought maybe I should check the rifle."

"The rifle is my concern."

"Lonnie . . ." he paused, then went on. "After all, you're only a girl. A man is better with a rifle."

I felt heat in my face. "You don't know the first thing about me, mister, yet you go claiming you're better than me. If there's one thing I'm not, it's helpless." I pointed toward the bedroom. "Go to bed."

He smiled. "No. Not yet. First I want something from you."

My hackles came up. "From me?" I asked coldly.

"I want to know your side of the story." He saw the refusal in my face and put up a hand to halt my quick words. "Lonnie, I told you my troubles. I only want the same treatment from you. Fair and square. I want to know what happened when your family was killed."

"You know as much as you need," I said woodenly.

He stroked the cat. "I'm only curious. I don't plan to argue about it with you. But some men never tell of getting shot, and you've got my story."

I had to admit to myself—grudgingly, of course—that he was right. But I couldn't understand his interest. What did it matter?

"Why do you want to know?"

He frowned, hunching his good shoulder. "I don't really know. But why would a girl stay out here by

55

herself when her whole family's been killed?"

The question took no special thought, and the answer came quickly, easily. "It's my home, Toby. My land. Would you pick up and leave something you loved if it was yours, free and clear?"

He smiled faintly, thoughtfully, still stroking the cat. "It would depend on what prodded me to leave." He looked me straight in the eye. "Tell me what happened. Call it an even trade. My tale for yours."

"I never counted stories as tradeable goods," I told him, pouring a bucket of water over the dirty dishes. I'd let them soak in the barrel and wash them later.

"Lonnie," he said softly, gently, "why weren't you killed with the rest?"

It crept across the room quietly, carefully, pulling an answer from me even though I'd rejected the demands before. My voice was hollow, not mine, but I was the one speaking. I sat down on the rag rug before the rocker and folded my legs beneath me, staring into my lap.

"Because I wasn't here. I'd run off. Against what my ma told me, for I was a girl always chasing daydreams rather then tending to my chores." I swallowed and lifted my eyes to his. "I really do understand why you left home, Toby. I understand what makes a man wander. I used to do it myself."

"Lonnie, maybe I shouldn't have asked you—"

"Maybe it's time I talked about it." I shrugged offhandedly. "I never have before." I took a deep breath. "Anyway, I survived the killings because I'd wandered off. I was left to carry on what my pa began, and I mean to do it."

"What happened?"

The old familiar guilt-pain clutched at my belly, sickening me. It was a pain I'd not felt for some time. I hadn't thought about the brutal murders for a long while, but memories of that day were as vivid in my head as if it had happened yesterday.

Still, I tried to keep my voice even and unemotional. "Like I said, I wandered off daydreaming. I went farther than ever before. I stayed longer than I'd been told. Then when I heard a scream, I started running."

"Away from it?"

I smiled crookedly. "No. To it. By the time I got back here the scavengers were gone. My ma, pa, sister and baby brother were all dead. The lean-to was on fire and the animals had been scattered. I tried to beat out the flames by myself for a long time, once I saw I could do nothing for my folks. Then men came from town, seeing the smoke on the wind. They found me."

"What happened, Lonnie?"

"I got sick."

"Just—sick?"

I refused to look at him, remembering my shame. "I couldn't sleep at night because of bad dreams. I couldn't eat. It was my fault, you see, because I wandered away." I shrugged. "Anyway—that's what I felt. Abner Barton and his wife kept me with them in town and looked after me. When I was better, I came home."

He swallowed. "When—how long ago did this happen?"

"I was fifteen. Just over two years ago."

"You've lived here alone that long?"

"It's what I chose to do," I said doggedly.

"But—a girl? A girl your age working a farm like this? It isn't possible."

Suddenly I was angrier than I ever had been before. This reaction was something I'd dealt with for a long time, but to hear it from him hurt me. He wasn't even giving me the benefit of the doubt, he just dismissed my words and denied me my accomplishments. Without a second thought.

"You're like all the rest, aren't you? Just like the others who stare at me and shake their heads, claiming I'm a lunatic and driven out of my head by pain and grief. It isn't like that, Toby! I do it because it's what I am. And I've done it for two years."

"How?"

I set my jaw and looked steadily at him. "I learned how to shoot my pa's rifle in case anyone else felt like bothering me, and for hunting. Me and the saddle mare learned how to plow a field and harvest it. We've got crooked furrows, maybe, but the corn don't mind. With the river there's plenty of water available, and I made the vegetable garden bigger. Other stuff I trade for in town, at the grocery." I shrugged. "I ain't saying it was easy, Toby, but I never figured it would be. It's a life." I smiled crookedly. "Mine."

His surprise was replaced by another emotion which galled me as much as outright disbelief. "Lonnie—"

"I don't want your pity! I want you healed and out of here."

He smiled and took up my challenge. "It's just hard to see you doing all this by yourself."

"A woman can do a man's work," I said flatly. "When it comes down to doing it."

"Maybe."

I flipped by braid behind my shoulder. "I've got nothing to prove to you. Choose to believe it or not, that's for you to decide. I know what I've done and that's all that matters to me."

He was interested and, I thought, compassionate. Maybe my words had gotten to him. "How have you managed?"

"Hard work, steady work."

He was all farmer now. "How many acres?"

"Forty. Most I let lie. I can't work the whole place, but enough to get by on."

"What have you got in the ground?"

"Corn. Vegetables. I've got meats stored in the springhouse, and plenty of poultry. I make a decent living."

He ruffled Patch's fur and then smoothed it all down again, staring into the distance. "With help you could put the whole farm to work. Turn a profit. It's good land."

"I know it's good. My pa picked it out with a lot of thought to what could be made of it. But I can't hire help. That takes money I don't have to spare. I don't want charity. This is a Ryan place. I'll work it myself."

Toby brought his intent blue eyes up from Patch to my face, searching me out. "Seventeen's marrying age. Past it for some girls. I expect you could have

59

found help without having to *hire* it."

I blushed fiery red but felt amused all the same. "There will be no man calling himself a husband here."

His black brows lanced down. The expression didn't suit the open, friendly cast of his face. "Why not? Every girl marries sooner or later. At least—she wants to."

"No," I said quietly. "This is mine, this land. I've already learned what it is to be valued for the land alone, thanks to one of the boys in town who wanted to marry me for the farm. I do just fine on my own. I need no one."

"The work could kill you."

"I'm strong. I know how to look after myself. Hard work only kills them who ain't fit for it. Use sense and you can get along fine for years—for a lifetime—and I intend to do it. I've got no worries here."

That was a challenge to him. "What if blight struck your corn?"

"I've got my garden."

"What if it goes under?"

"I've got back supplies stored away. And—" I lifted a hand to halt his words—"I've got a rifle and I'm a fair shot with it. I could shoot my supper. Nothing will drive me from this land."

"Not even Barstows?"

Our eyes met across the room, steady and set on both sides. It was a strange moment, as if we'd exchanged thoughts and feelings and found one another stronger than we'd expected. Maybe there was some grit to Toby Markham after all.

I grinned to myself. I already knew the weight of my sand. I smiled across at Toby. "No. Not even Barstows."

Toby at last went back to bed, worn out to the bone. I made certain he was settled, noting he fell deeply asleep almost instantly, then I went out to hoe the cornfield.

Tracker came along and cast about for any scents he might turn up. I slapped at his tail as I lugged the wooden hoe up the hill to the cornfield, and smiled contentedly as I traversed the land. The acres stretching before me meant security, and I respected it accordingly.

Tender green sprouts were up, breaking through the rich soil. The cottonwood tree standing sentinel over the corner of the field dripped white fluff, and some of the streamers sailed away on breezes to land in other fields. Weeds already crept into the plowed furrows, encroaching on the new corn shoots, so I set the hoe to the ground and began to work.

The day was warm, beading sweat on my forehead and running down my temples. My thin dress already stuck to my back. I cleared the field carefully, intent on my work, digging out the stubborn weeds by hand to make certain the corn shoots had half a chance to reach full growth. It was hard work, sure enough, as I'd told Toby, but the kind of work I found pleasure in. It felt good to be out with the sky and the sun and the plains.

I heard the horse snort and jerked upright,

clenching the hoe tightly in callused palms. Tracker, I thought abstractedly, Tracker's at the river. Up-wind.

"Good day to you, miss," said the bounty hunter, tipping his hat.

Fear leaped in my chest. I fought it back down and stared up at him on his dun horse with what I hoped was a suitably innocent expression.

"You back for any particular reason?" I asked.

He studied me, smiling in an odd manner. His eyes were greenish, now he was close enough for me to see him clearly. His hair, beneath his stained gray hat, was sandy-colored. I placed him somewhere near forty years of age, but I couldn't tell which side.

"I'm doing my job, miss," he said. "Following tracks."

"Tracks," I said blankly.

His face, darkened by weatherburn, creased in a smile. "The ones leading here, miss. The ones I didn't see before because you kept me on the far side of the river."

"I didn't keep you there. I just didn't invite you onto my land." I shielded my eyes against the sun's glare. "I have every right to keep people off my land."

He shifted in the saddle, hands resting on the saddle horn. "I reckon you do. Now, why don't you tell me who it is you're hiding."

"I'm hiding no one."

He sighed and pushed his hat back on his head. "Miss, I'm not here to harm you. Once I was a lawman, like I said, and I don't intend to break the law by meaning you harm. You have no need to be

62

afraid of me.''

"I'm not."

"You're afraid of something.''

I gripped the hoe firmly. "I think you'd better go.''

"Not before you tell me who you're hiding.''

I swallowed and edged away from him, figuring to turn and run when I had the chance. He read it in my eyes.

"This old pony's done a lot of things, miss, one of which was learning to cut cattle. I reckon he can cut you just as well.''

"You're on my property," I said, shaking with anger. "Get off it!"

He kneed the horse closer to me. I felt the animal's warm breath on my neck as he snorted, pulling irritably at restraining reins.

"Cutting pony, are you?" I asked myself, smiling grimly. Silently I apologized to the innocent animal, then brought the hoe up sharply. It whacked the horse in the nose and shot his head in the air as he jerked back in pain. I ran.

I heard the man curse. I threw the hoe away, realizing it might hinder my flight. Breathlessly I tried to whistle for Tracker, but no sound escaped my lips. I heard the pounding hooves behind me, then fell beneath the heavy body as it hurtled down from above.

It hurt, but I scrambled out from under him and shouted for the dog. I heard the answering bell, but before I could start running again the man's hand closed on my ankle. He jerked me down.

"Damn it, missy, stay still long enough so I can get

my wind back," he wheezed. "I don't want to hurt you."

Since he effectively held me prisoner, I gave up my flight. I stared at him angrily as we sat tangled together on the ground. I was scraped and bruised from the tumble, and I hoped he was equally so.

"That was a pretty mean trick to pull on my old pony," he said. "Hitting him in the nose with a hoe handle."

"I couldn't reach *you*."

He laughed, brushing grit and dust from his clothing. He resettled his hat and studied me, a smile creeping from beneath the big mustache he wore.

"Now, miss . . ." he began, but stopped as Tracker arrived, hackled and snarling.

I grinned at him triumphantly. "You'd best let me go. Tracker doesn't much care for men who jump on me from a running horse."

He released me with alacrity, taking care to remain very still. Tracker circled him warily as I brushed grass and dirt from my dress, feeling a scrape on my left cheekbone. I got up and moved to the horse, who obliged me by standing still as I relieved him of the rifle and turned it on its owner.

"Well now, supposing you tell me the truth for a change. Who are you?"

"Dan Michael Loggins," he said with a strange dignity. "From Missouri."

"Bounty hunter," I mocked.

"Now," he agreed.

"Don't lie to me."

He placed a hand over his heart. "I wouldn't dream of it, miss. Particularly in view of that highly effective weapon you persist in aiming in my direction."

"You deserve it," I said, wiping at a sore spot on my nose. "Jumping down on me like that."

"I had to do something," he protested. "You were getting away."

"Thought that horse of yours was a cutting pony. Surely a girl don't pose much problem to him."

He smiled wryly. "You plumb knocked any notion of cutting clear out of his jugheaded skull, little lady. Whapping him like that."

I gestured, done with that. "Tell me the truth. Who are you?"

"I've told you once. You won't get it again." His green eyes were worried. "Do you truly know how to shoot my rifle?"

"Of course I do. If you'd like a demonstration, I could shoot that hat off your head."

"No," he said hastily, "that won't be necessary. I'll forgo the demonstration."

I stared at him hard, trying to fit any Barstow characteristic to him. Trouble was, I didn't know much. But he worried me, though I didn't dare tell him my suspicions. Naming him a Barstow to his face would show him I knew what had happened. And that, logically, would lead him straight to Toby.

"What are you out here for?"

"I'm looking for someone," he said. "Like I told you."

"*That* might be true," I agreed grimly. "Who?"

He glared at me. "Matt Barstow and his gang. As if you didn't know. I'm willing to bet one of them is holed up in that farmhouse, right now."

I stared at him blankly, then opened my mouth to deny his statement. But I said nothing as Toby came walking up the rise. He was still shirtless, but wore his boots and carried my rifle. I stared at him.

"I heard you yell for Tracker," he explained. "I thought you were in trouble."

"Nothing I can't handle," I said dryly, staring down at my prisoner. "I caught myself a Barstow."

"*I'm* not a Barstow!" Dan Michael Loggins exclaimed, staring at Toby. "Who are you?"

"He's no Barstow," I said wearily. "He's the man hiding in my house."

Loggins cursed with great inventiveness. "I would've sworn I had one of the Barstows cornered."

"No," said Toby, "just me. And you're lucky I can say for certain you're not one of them, either. Otherwise Lonnie might have shot you."

Loggins removed his hat and rubbed a hand through his hair disgustedly. "So all this is for nothing. I've lost two days because of you. A nobody."

"Not exactly a nobody," I told him. "Toby's wanted, right enough, but not by the law. By the Barstows themselves."

"Why?" Loggins asked quietly, staring fixedly at Toby.

"You're a former lawman," I said. "Surely you know who testified against Ben Barstow."

"Some kid from Minnesota," the bounty hunter answered. "Some kid who wanted to be a buffalo hunter."

Toby grinned at me. "See? I told you the truth."

"So you did," I said wearily, dropping my

66

borrowed rifle to my side. "Let's go in the house and talk this over."

"The dog?" asked Dan Michael Loggins.

"Tracker, let him up. He may be stupid, but he's not worth wasting your teeth over." I grinned at the disgruntled expression on the man's face. "Come along, mister."

He came.

Chapter Four

The lawman-turned-bounty-hunter walked into my house like he owned it. I nearly said something to him about it, then let it go. There were more important things to talk about. But it grated on me to see him stride into my house, drop his hat over a door-peg, and stand in the middle of the room surveying everything.

Toby held himself well going in, but I saw the strain underneath. He was far from being a well man. Still, I said nothing. If he wanted to make Loggins think he was healthy, I'd not interfere.

Trouble was, Loggins didn't miss much. He looked at Toby, then at me, and smiled.

"Wouldn't take much for me to get the upper hand, here, would it? Saying I was a Barstow, which I'm not." He shook his head. "A sick boy and a half-grown girl."

"Don't risk your silver on it," Toby said quietly. "Lonnie and I have the guns, and that old hound would light into you real quick if you tried anything."

"Maybe so," Loggins answered, scratching at his mustache, "but I reckon I still might come out ahead. Training and all."

"As a lawman?" I asked mockingly.

He nodded. "I was one of the best."

"So why'd you quit?"

His face was grim. "Barstow trouble, miss. If you'll invite me to sit a spell, I'll gladly explain it all to you."

I considered it a moment, then nodded. "Find yourself a seat."

Loggins did so, pulling up a chair and seating himself carefully as Tracker eyed him suspiciously. Poor hound, he'd had his fill of strangers lately.

Toby returned my rifle to its pegs by the door and took his place in the rocker. He did it smoothly, easing himself down as if he weren't troubled, but the pallor of his face and shadowed eyes gave him away. And Loggins knew it.

I sat down on the bench by the table and set the borrowed rifle next to me, in easy reach. I wasn't quite sure I trusted him yet.

"I'm hunting the Barstows," Dan Michael Loggins said quietly. "First I did it because I was a sheriff sworn to do it as a duty for Missouri, all legallike. It's still legal, for all that; I'm just not part of the law anymore. But I first started tracking them with a posse."

"This is Kansas," I pointed out. "What's a Missouri sheriff doing here?"

He looked affronted. "Kansas isn't the only state with Barstow trouble. Once or twice they've crossed

69

the line, and they've killed honest folk from Missouri. But you're right in part—my jurisdiction quit at the line." He shrugged. "As a sheriff I couldn't devote all my time to them, there were other things to do, so I put off my badge and came after them."

"For the money?" Toby asked.

Loggins rubbed at his mustache. "Partly. The reward's more than my yearly salary. I'd sure like to be the one who got it. But it's also a matter of pride. No one has caught them before, save for Ben, and I'd like to do it."

"You make it sound easy," I told him.

He shook his head. "I don't mean to. It ain't. They're hard men, miss, and need killing."

"And you're the man to do it?"

He grinned widely, green eyes glinting with amusement. "You don't think much of me, do you? Well, it don't matter. I reckon I'll find out when I catch up to them."

"You intend to just shoot them down, do you?" I asked scathingly. "Like animals?"

His good humor faded and the eyes were level and hard. "It's what they are, girl. Animals. They need culling from the herd, like a renegade steer in a bunch of prime beef."

I shivered in response to his tone. "But they're not around here. Why should they be?"

Loggins stared across at Toby. "You've got the witness who testified against Ben hidden here, girl. Where else do you think they'd be?"

I swallowed. "Those tracks you say you followed.

They led here?"

"Near enough," Loggins answered. "I couldn't be certain, but after you were so defensive at the river I decided to swing back and check things out. Thought there might be a possibility you were hiding one of the Barstows."

Toby smiled wanly. "No. She's just hiding me."

I met Toby's eyes across the room and saw the tired smile in them. "You belong in bed, Toby," I said. "You'll not heal if you keep wearing yourself out."

"Caught yourself a bullet, did you?" Loggins asked with interest.

Toby nodded. "Matt Barstow's got a powerful calling card. Even from a distance."

I walked to Toby and gestured. "Come on. Time to change your bandages."

Loggins rose. "Let me do it. I've had more experience at it than you."

I stared at him defiantly. "This is my house, mister. I'll do the tending. You just stay put where Tracker can keep an eye on you."

"Still don't trust me, do you?"

"Why should I? You could be lying to me. You could have made the whole story up." I smiled humorlessly at him. "Toby says you're not a Barstow, but has he really seen them close enough to be certain?"

Toby struggled to his feet. "I said he wasn't Lonnie. He isn't. Not him."

He reeled suddenly and Loggins caught him before he fell. I flashed the man a furious glance and grabbed hold of Toby's arm, but Loggins merely

71

brushed me aside and half-carried a protesting Toby into the bedroom. I followed sullenly, angry at the man's actions, but also worried about Toby.

He hadn't fainted again, but he was close to it. The strain of getting up and coming after Loggins outside had taken its toll on him. He was half-awake, mumbling something I couldn't understand. Loggins settled him on the bed, stripped his boots off and dropped them to the floor. He shot a hard glance at me.

"I reckon you got bandages. Get them."

I did, white-faced with resentment, and watched as the man gently tended Toby's wounded shoulder. It already looked better, clean, with reduced festering and swelling. Loggins nodded and tied off the bandage efficiently.

"You'll do," he told Toby, whose eyes were half-lidded and dazed. "You need rest and solid food, but you'll do."

"Lonnie?" Toby whispered.

"I'm here. Go to sleep."

"He'll be all right," Loggins said confidently, rising to tower over me.

I shrugged, ill-humored. "It's nothing to me. I don't rightly want him to die in my house, but he's nothing more than a stranger I'm tending to."

"I see." He grinned. "You got some coffee? I could sure use some."

I followed him from the bedroom into the front room again, disliking his familiarity. "You're not a guest, mister. Just a stranger who forced his way in here. I owe no hospitality to you."

72

"Then I'll help myself." He went to the cupboards and began searching through them.

I picked up his rifle. "You'd best go now, mister. You've worn out any welcome you might have gotten from me."

Loggins paused, staring at me. "Miss, I hate to do this to you, but if you keep on that way I'll have to. Gun or no, I'd still be able to stop you from doing me violence. I've never known a woman yet who could shoot a man face on."

"Would you like to try it from the receiving end?"

He grinned, then laughed aloud. Tracker, at my side, growled and took a step forward. Loggins held out a big hand, displaying strong fingers and a wide palm.

"I could stop that hound if it came to it, missy. He might take a hunk of hide off me, but I'd still choke him down. I've done it before."

"My name is Lonnie," I said between gritted teeth, realizing he spoke the truth, "and if you hurt that dog I'll shoot you down for certain."

Loggins nodded. "Fair deal, Lonnie. Now, can I have some coffee?"

I gave up. There was something about the man that diminished another person. He was big and strong, but it wasn't just physical presence. He had a force in his character as well, and even I had to answer it. I hated it, but I answered it.

Once he had his cup of coffee, he settled down in the rocker. Patch came in the open front door, took one look at him, then headed for the bedroom like a shot. Loggins stared after the cat quizzically.

"He likes Toby," I explained.

The big man sipped at his coffee and slid his eyes over the room. He saw the faded photographs of my family on the wall and the little round table with the lacy white cloth holding some of my ma's trinkets. The fancy Frenchified clock on the mantle ticked loudly in the silence, and then he looked back at me.

"You alone here?"

I sat at the table and nursed my own coffee. "I am. You got something to say about it?"

"I reckon not. What happened?"

"Nothing of your concern," I said.

He grinned crookedly beneath the mustache. "I reckon it isn't. Just curious."

I said nothing, and he continued staring at me over the rim of his cup. "How long?"

"Two years."

He nodded. "I see it in your eyes. Long enough to make it work, barely. Long enough to make you realize the folly in it."

"Folly!" I slammed my cup down on the table, slopping coffee across the wood. "It ain't a folly!"

Loggins jerked his head toward the bedroom. "Maybe he'll stay on with you awhile. Make the place run better."

"He'll be gone soon enough, I'll see to that. I don't need help, mister. I do fine by myself."

"Lonnie," he said sorrowfully, "working a farm alone is hard enough for a man. For a woman—well, it can't go on forever. One day, you'll need help."

"Not me."

74

"You will, you know."

"Not me."

He finished the coffee and rose, retrieving his hat and setting the empty cup on the table next to mine. "Fair enough." He walked out of the house.

I sat stunned for a moment, staring after him, then ran to the door with his gun. "You forgot your rifle!"

He turned. "Oh, I'm not leaving yet. Just seeing to my horse."

I gaped at him in astonishment. "You're not *staying* here!"

"For a spell. Just long enough to see if the Barstows plan on showing up."

"It's *my* house!"

He grinned and tipped his hat. "Thank you kindly for the invite, ma'am. I accept with pleasure."

I stared after him, shaking with frustration, then turned and went back in the house. There was no arguing with that man.

Toby was sleeping deeply when I looked in on him, and I almost envied him his chance to lose worries and concerns in sleep. Only three days before I'd had nothing more pressing to do than routine chores; now I had a sick man on my hands and another man I heartily wished was sick.

Dan Michael Loggins, whose name fascinated me for its oddity, was a puzzle. He'd told me a part of his past but his future was left unclear. Nothing he said set my mind at rest. He was here, he said, to wait for the Barstows.

I asked him what he'd do if they never came. He grinned and said he'd just ride on, as I undoubtedly longed for him to do, and when I agreed he laughed.

"But they'll come, Lonnie," he said to me as he sat at the table and cleaned his rifle.

"How can you be so sure?"

He worked carefully, oiling the bits and pieces of the machinery that made the weapon work. "Men like them don't give up. I'm not saying they *know* he's here, but they won't leave it to chance. They'll come."

I stood at the stove, baking biscuits for supper. "I'm not afraid of them."

Loggins smiled oddly at me over his gun. "You must be the only soul who isn't. And you're just a bit of a girl, too."

My teeth clenched. "I'm neither ignorant nor stupid, girl or not. I know it means danger, mister, but it's something I'll face. Wouldn't you in my place?"

"I'd never let myself be in your place, Lonnie, were I a girl."

I stirred at the dough viciously. "Just goes to show you've got no grit."

"You'll have me believing you've got enough for the both of us."

"Maybe I do. Listen, I know Matt Barstow won't give up until he finds Toby. But I'll make certain he doesn't find him here."

"Matt Barstow will beat the grass for him, Lonnie. Better yet, he'll burn it. Will you give Toby up to him?"

"I won't turn a sick man out. Not to anyone."

"I'm not saying you should. And I'd be mighty grateful to you for tending me, in his place. What I'm saying is—you'd be better off in town."

"I'm staying."

Loggins set aside his tools and looked at me levelly. "Lonnie, these are outlaws I'm speaking of. Not dandified, glorified heroes out of those dime novels. These are dangerous men."

I smiled grimly at him. "You sound like you know them."

"Enough of them, I know. I've spent a year tracking them. I know their habits. I know what kind of men they are."

I left my biscuits to bake and walked to the rocker, settling down in it with my legs tucked under me. Loggins watched me silently, pensively, puzzled by my actions. I lifted my head and smiled.

"What kind of men are they, then? Tell me what you know."

"Why do you want to hear this?"

"So I know what to expect if they come."

He sighed and returned to his rifle, shaking his head. "It's no glory-tale, girl. Matt Barstow's a man with intelligence, and he uses it to fatten his pockets with stolen money. He and his brother started raiding and robbing and did it on their own for a few years, then met up with Wes Lacklander. He's probably the worst of the bunch."

"I'd have thought Matt was. Smarts and outlawry sound dangerous."

His eyes flicked to me, hard and cold. "Matt

Barstow, for all his killing and thieving, is still a man with normal appetites. Lacklander isn't."

I felt oddly chilled. "What do you mean?"

"You'd be better off not knowing."

"Why?" I tugged reflectively at my braid. "I want to know it all."

His face was stiff, distant. "Then I'll lay it all out so you can look at it. You won't like it. Wes Lacklander isn't right in the head. He craves killing and women, and often they go hand in hand."

"I—I don't understand."

"He likes to have a woman before he kills, and after, and sometimes he kills the woman when he's done with her." He stared at me expressionlessly. "Now, are you satisfied?"

I swallowed convulsively, bitter gall souring my mouth. The idea sickened me, but I refused to show my revulsion to Loggins. Instead I nodded.

"Go on. There's more, ain't there?"

He sighed. "There's Jordy Macklin."

"I know a little about him." I shrugged at his glance of surprise. "Jordy's pa founded this county. News of Jordy travels fast."

"He left home still wet behind the ears, bound and determined to cause trouble for his father. He's done it, too."

"Who's the fourth man?"

"Rooster Gibbs. Carries a knife. He's older than them all, and he's been in this business a long time. It's said he's a match for any gunman with his blade."

I stared blankly across the room. "And now they

want to kill Toby."

"He got Ben hanged, Lonnie."

I sighed and rubbed at my jaw, feeling the knurled scar curving up my chin. "It must be hard for him, knowing what he faces. He's twenty years old, and already nearly killed by a murdering bunch of white men."

"So, it was white men who killed your folks."

I jerked upright. "How would you know that?"

"Your voice. You show no surprise at what the Barstows are capable of. Sounds like you've suffered at the hands of men very like them. Not Indians."

"It might be easier if it had been," I told him bluntly. "Easier to explain away than knowing white men murdered folk of their own kind."

He snapped the last piece of his rifle into place. "Lonnie, dead is dead." He smiled grimly. "Regardless who does the killing."

I looked into his green eyes and silently admitted he was right. I said nothing to him, keeping it to myself. But he knew all the same.

"You'd best to into town and tell the sheriff."

"I can't."

"Too stubborn?"

"Ridgely hasn't got a sheriff. It's too small. There's no railroad spur, no beef ranches. Just a place farmers go for supplies."

"I went through there," he said, nodding. "I recall there's not much to occupy a man. Two saloons, though."

"There's no need for a sheriff. If a farmer gets drunk and gets too rowdy, he gets heaved into a shed and locked in overnight. That's our jail." I shrugged.

"There's never been a murder . . . except for my folks."

"There might be another one now."

I met his look. "No. Not here. Not Toby."

Slowly he smiled. "I admire your confidence."

I rose and left the room, seeing to Toby.

Chapter Five

He smiled up at me from the big bed. "The sleep did me good. I feel better."

"Supper's ready. Let me get some."

"Is he still here?" Toby asked sharply.

I twisted my mouth. "I can't get rid of him. He says he's staying until he's certain the Barstows aren't coming."

Toby sighed and ran a hand through his hair. "Even if he were here when they came, they'd still outnumber us."

"Us?"

He stared up at me. "You don't mean to face them alone, do you?"

"I hope not to face them at all. There's no certainty they'll come."

He released a hard breath. "I hope not. I surely hope not."

"Let me get you supper."

"Wait." He grinned beguilingly at me as I turned back. "Will you eat in here with me?"

"I've eaten."

His face fell. "Oh, well—at least sit with me. Please?"

"You've got a powerful thirst for company."

"I enjoy sparring with you." He grinned. "Like a barefisted boxer I saw once. But you do it with words."

I scowled at him. "You've got a way of twisting words yourself, Toby Markham."

"Lonnie, just sit with me. It won't kill you."

"I guess not," I agreed, and went off to fetch his supper.

Loggins sat at the table with a lantern at his elbow, poring over some papers. He only grunted when I asked him what they were, so I let him be. It wasn't like me to ask in the first place, so I was just as happy he ignored the question. I gathered up stew, biscuits and coffee for Toby and went into the bedroom with Tracker following.

He ate well, though fast, and I had to make him slow down. He grinned with stew smeared on his chin and shook his head.

"You cook a good meal, Lonnie."

"It's only stew and biscuits."

"Maybe it's because I'm so hungry."

I grunted. "Likely so. But slow down or you'll choke."

He ate more slowly when the edge was off his hunger, and began to question me again. Like Loggins, he thought the sheriff in Ridgely should be informed of our troubles. I sighed resignedly and once more explained the lack.

"No law at all?" he whispered, stunned.

"No one has to know you're here," I told him. "Least of all the Barstow gang. I never say much when I go to town, so it won't look as though I'm hiding anything. If Matt and his boys come through there's nothing anyone can pass on. They'll just leave."

He shook his head, setting the empty plate and mug on the bedside table. "No, they'll know. They'll know I'm here somewhere. A wounded man can't get far. If they're as dangerous as I think, they might tear this place apart just looking for me."

"No one would ever think of me as being the one looking after you," I said quietly, perching on the chair. "Not Lonnie Ryan."

He looked at me curiously. "How can you be so certain?"

I smiled crookedly. "You don't know me, Toby. You don't understand how it is. I've made things the way they are, and I work to keep them this way."

"You're right, I don't understand. What are you talking about?"

I fussed with the curling tips of my braid, avoiding his searching eyes. "You see, I'm not the friendliest soul in these parts. I haven't done anything to change it, either. For a reason. I don't deny that what I'm doing is odd for a girl, so I leave it known I want no interference. That way no one bothers me. The townfolk—well, they just shake their heads and let me go on my way." I slid him a quick look, then glanced away again. "I'm strange, Toby, or so they say. Too much a solitary soul. They'd *never* expect this of me, and I'm not the one to tell them any different."

He couldn't accept it. "Why do you risk so much for me? All I've brought you is trouble. If I stay here, you could get hurt."

83

I shrugged carelessly, dropping the braid. "Nothing has hurt me yet. I don't plan on letting anything get to me, now or later. It's like I said before."

"What is?"

"I'd do the same for a hurt critter." I grinned at his disgruntled expression, then laughed aloud. "Of course most of *them* know better than to tangle with the Barstow gang."

He picked at the quilt. "How soon do you think they'll come?"

"*If* they come," I said. "And I don't know."

I picked up his dirty dishes and went back to the kitchen, preparing to clean up. Loggins had also eaten well, and I had more dishes than usual to clean. It was odd having so many mouths to feed after only my own, but I was willing to shoulder the burden. For a while.

As I worked I thought on the idea of having a sheriff to handle law troubles like this. A sheriff sounded particularly appealing when I thought about the Barstows. I sincerely wished we had a strong man with grit enough to serve as lawman.

I cast over people in my head. Abner Barton: the burly blacksmith who had so kindly taken me in after the murders. I had been made part of his family and he'd always treated me as a daughter rather than as a temporary visitor. Barton was a strong man I respected and genuinely liked, but he believed in letting individuals rule themselves, rather than setting himself in charge. He would never agree to act as sheriff.

Elmer Tolleson owned the dry goods store, and I counted him another good man with strong convictions. But Tolleson, a Virginian, had come to Kansas from the Civil War. He had bid his final goodbyes to weapons. I doubted he would ever accept the position, especially with Barstows involved. Tolleson was no coward, but had seen his fill of killing. A sheriff might possibly bait such men into acting rashly. Tolleson would never let himself be that man.

I thought of Mick, the stout Irishman who ran the biggest saloon. Mick could wield a shotgun with the best of them and was never one to accept trouble quietly, but he preferred his fists over real weapons. A roistering brawler, no matter how handy with his fists, would never gain approval as sheriff.

That left Olaf Larsson, called the Swede by all who knew him. Larsson owned the mercantile and grocery, a peaceable man who brought his wife and baby son from Sweden to settle in the New Land. But he'd lost both son and wife to sickness and he'd never married again. He ran his store quietly with great fairness and compassion; he always gave me more than enough credit for the tradeable goods I brought in. Olaf Larsson was one of the reasons I survived. But sadness reflected in his kindly blue eyes and stooped shoulders and though folks went to him for sound advice, he was not a lawman.

Good men all, but not the sort to take a solid stand against scavenger outlaws like the Barstows. Not many would.

I looked back at Dan Michael Loggins, still lost in his mass of papers, and wondered at his former occupation. Had he really been a lawman? Had he been good at it? Would he be trustworthy in a fight?

I shook such thoughts off. Loggins would stay for

a spell, then he'd leave, wanting only to chase down the Barstows. He'd never dream of aiding a town against the gang, and certainly not me. His reasons for fighting the Barstows were purely financial.

"What are you staring at, girl?" he rumbled from the table.

"Nothing."

"I can feel your great eyes burning a hole through my head. You're thinking something."

"All right. About you. I'm wondering what sort of a man you are. Good? Bad? Cowardly? Brave?" I grinned at his astonished expression. "It's true, I do sometimes think about things. I'm not a machine doing daily toil without thought. I'm human enough, God knows."

Loggins straightened one side of his mustache. "I know you're no machine, my girl. There's a woman in that slender body of yours."

I felt my face turn fiery red. "That has nothing to do with the conversation!"

He smiled. "I'm old enough to be your father, girl. I'm hardly harboring lewd thoughts in my head."

I turned my back on him, ready to ignore him until I could face myself again, but his voice continued. There was an odd note in it, a reminiscence, and I listened closely as I washed the dishes.

"You're a lot like her, you know. Proud and defiant, ready to deny God himself if you're set on something. My Charlotte was the same, before the hours killed her."

I froze at the wash-barrel, then turned slowly to face him. "Your wife?"

He shrugged lightly. "I had one once. We came out

86

to Missouri for me to be a deputy, and later I became the sheriff. I worked hard, long hours, and Charlotte finally got tired of it all."

"You said—you said she was dead."

His sandy brows lifted. "Did I say that? Well, she isn't. She wasn't." He sighed. "She took off with a railroad man who could give her the time she wanted."

"So you fastened your mind on chasing the Barstows, to leave it all behind," I said to myself. But I kept it silent. It wouldn't do for him to see I gave him a compassionate thought.

Loggins stared at me past the flickering light of the lantern. "But you're really not like her at all. It was just a passing thought."

I said nothing, and turned back again to my dishes.

Breakfast was an odd affair. Before it had always been me alone at the table; now there were two hungry men waiting for what I offered. I resigned myself to it and cooked bigger meals, and saw to it they had enough to keep them going.

Toby was healing fast. Already he was up and moving around, discussing things with Loggins at great length. Mostly I let them talk and did my chores.

It was strange how they made me talk. It wasn't forced from me, exactly, but I'd found it was hard to ignore two pairs of curious eyes fixed on me when a question was asked. I'd grown used to saying nothing other than a word or two to Tracker or Patch; now I felt wrong in keeping silent all the time.

But the two of them talked enough for a houseful of folks.

Loggins, to give him his due, offered to help me with the chores. I dismissed his intent as manners, but refused him. It wouldn't do, I explained, to have a stranger show his face around my farm. Not when I'd never kept any before. He agreed, and gave himself up to a life of leisure. I wondered if he'd really meant the offer.

Toby, on the other hand, was genuine. I could see it troubled him to be so helpless, though each day his strength improved. No longer did he keep to his bed, and he roamed the house like a caged lion. He and Loggins spent the hours swapping tall tales, and I grinned silently to myself as I heard them and went about my work.

I scattered grain in the henhouse and watched as the hens got off their eggs to scratch and peck at the corn kernels and grain. Three different crops of chicks scurried around the dirt, avoiding pecks from the ruddy rooster who called the domain his own.

The brown mare, when I got to her, greeted me with a soft nicker. I ran my fingers down her neck and slipped my other hand under her jaw to rub the firm layer of muscles lying quiescent beneath her silken skin. She stretched out her head, eyes gone heavy-lidded, asking for more.

Sadly, I saw her grown older, aged, graying around her nostrils and over her eyes where the hollowed pockets sank deeper with each year. She still had great heart and a willingness to work, though her intent had been perverted. Originally she'd been my pa's saddle mare in Ohio. She'd known only the touch of his hands and a snaffle in her mouth; now she served as my work animal. She didn't seem to mind much, but I wondered sadly if she missed the freedom of the plains, loping along with the wind against her face and the breeze whipping her mane and tail.

I looped my arm upwards about her throat, hooking fingers into the thick mane at the crest of her neck. I tugged gently, then slid my other hand up to stroke her muzzle. She blew softly at me, hot horse breath caressing my hand. I loved the smell of the lean-to, and found peace with my animals. The mare nickered at me again and shoved at my hand, hungry. I let her go and patted her shoulder.

"All right, mare, I'll feed you. I guess you've put up with me long enough."

Princess also was tugging at her tie-rope by now, hungry and impatient, so I forked fodder to them both. The cow's sides bulged with calf and her udder was distended though I'd milked her only an hour before. A heifer, I said to myself, please let it be a heifer.

Furry warmth engulfed my ankles. Patch wove a courtship around me, talking up a storm. He knew the cow meant milk and occasionally I gave in to his delicate persuasion and squirted him a warm stream straight out of the udder. He posted himself in an accessible spot and waited. I knelt by the cow's side and took one of her teats, watching the tom. The very tip of his tongue appeared.

His patience was unbearable. At last I gave in and worked the teat. I aimed for his mouth but the first stream hit him square between the eyes. He didn't complain. He just sat up on his haunches like a dog, front paws dangling, and raised his mouth to milk level.

Tracker caught up to me as I went down to the springhouse, trotting along with head slung low as he searched for interesting scents. I caught his tail as he trotted by and he sent a belling bark kiting to the sky. I thought it a fitting sound for the bright morning, a rich noise filling the cottonwood grove. Warm sunlight filtered through the trees, painting greens and golds across the grass. It was a clean-smelling morning as dew-damp grass bent beneath my feet. I liked the feeling of fresh wetness against my bare legs and feet. Tracker nearly bowled me over, then I sent him on his way.

The ground around the springhouse, built low near the river, was slick and slimy with wetness. Tracker's prints were imbedded there with my own. I cut down a haunch of venison and tucked it under my arm, planning on a tasty meal for supper. And more biscuits. They both liked my biscuits.

I was nearly to the house when I saw the horse and rider coming over the hill. Down my road. It led directly to my door, and there was no mistaking the rider intended to come calling.

He still had some ground to cover, not moving quickly, so I walked swiftly inside to set down my meat and gather up the rifle.

Toby was at the door as I came in; Loggins was seated in the rocker working at his pipe. I didn't waste a minute fetching down my gun, or giving orders.

"Get in the bedroom, both of you. Quick."

Loggins straightened in the rocker. "Why? Who's coming?"

"A rider. I can't tell who yet. Get in the bedroom and close the door. I'll handle this."

Toby wanted to protest but Loggins wasted no time. "Come on. We'd best do as she says. It's her deal."

A moment later they had shut themselves in the bedroom and I looked swiftly around the house to see if anything would give my visitors away. Loggins had taken his papers with him and Toby had nothing, so I had nothing to hide. The dun horse was tied on the far side of the house, away from the brown mare who'd taken a dislike to him, so I didn't think Loggins' horse would give us away.

I heard Tracker barking, loping in from the trees. Patch slipped between my legs and took his post beneath the rocker. I went to the open doorway and stood, rifle resting easy in my arms.

As the rider came down off the hill and into the dirt yard I relaxed, dropping the rifle to set on its stock with my hand wrapped around the barrel. It was Abner Barton come calling, not a man to fret about.

Barton reined in his sorrel horse and raised a hand in greeting, smiling down at me. "Mornin', Lonnie."

"Mornin'. Step down and water your horse."

He dismounted and moved to the well to crank up the bucket. He set it out for the horse to drink from, keeping it steady so the animal wouldn't upset it.

He was a heavy-set man, not fat, but muscled, a bull of a man grown big from blacksmithing over

91

long years. He wore work clothes: heavy boots, faded trousers, sweat-stained shirt with the sleeves rolled back, and a dusty black hat. His forearms were big, brawny with iron-hard muscles.

I could see the old, ugly scar on his right arm, a smith's telltale brand: a bite from an angry horse. He removed his hat and I saw the balding head burned permanently red-brown from the sun and the heat of his smithy.

I wondered what had brought him here.

He waited until his horse had watered before dipping up a drink for himself. He was like that; for him the animals came first, especially the horses. His gelding was a fine animal. Not classy, perhaps, but solid-built, stout, glossy with good health and special care.

I propped my rifle against the bench beside the door and went forward, tossing my braid behind my back.

"What brings you out here today? You've not been by here for a spell."

He nodded, sending the bucket back to the depths of the well. His reins dropped and the sorrel nuzzled the ground, lipping for salt and minerals in the earth.

Barton stood favoring his bad leg, left crooked from a break he'd suffered years before from the kick of a horse. He'd suffered his share of horse-caused hurts, but he loved them still. Horses were in his blood as much as the land was in mine.

"Lonnie, I meant to come sooner. I meant to make certain you're all right out here. But things got piled up at the smithy, and I've been kept pretty busy. Now

I have a reason for coming. It concerns the farm."

I grew very quiet. "What farm?"

"Yours, Lonnie."

Something in his tone turned me cold. I nodded. "You'd best come in."

Barton sat at the table and I took my seat across from him. Tracker settled on the floor next to me, but I saw he watched the closed door to the bedroom more than Abner Barton. I hoped the dog wouldn't act suspicious because Barton was a smart man. He'd realize something was up.

"Well," I said uneasily, "speak your piece."

He sighed. "You know I admire what you've done here. And I know how much you want to stay, and how determined you are to make the farm work."

"It's my home."

"Don't you think it might be better if you came to live with Emily and myself in town? She loves you like a daughter, and so do I. The boys would like to have a sister." He sounded horribly uncomfortable, but his words were sincere.

I took in a heavy breath, trying to figure out what had gone wrong. This wasn't like him. He knew me well, though he didn't understand some of my feelings, and he hadn't brought this subject up for a long time.

"Mr. Barton, you and your wife offered this to me before," I said, carefully polite. "I know you meant well by it then, and now. But there's no need for it. I'm content here." I looked at him levelly. "You know that."

He picked his way through what he wanted to say. I knew him as a forthright man and it made me wonder all the more what he was driving at. Whatever it was, he didn't like it much.

"Lonnie, Emily and I simple want you to know you have a place to go."

"I'm not going anywhere."

He swallowed and removed his hat, dropping it on the table with finality. His blue eyes, meeting mine, were painfully sincere. "Lonnie, you must leave."

A coldness settled deep in the pit of my belly. I nearly shivered from it, then ignored it and straightened on the bench. I smiled at him steadily.

"Now why would I be leaving here? This is my home. I belong here. No place else."

He rubbed a big-knuckled hand across his face, brows furrowed deeply. "You must understand. There's a chance—a chance the farm may not be yours at all. Lonnie—I know how this sounds. I know what it means to hear this. But—you must understand. Emily and I want you to come to us."

I was struck dumb with astonishment and shock, unable to push a word past the constriction in my throat. For a long moment we stared at one another across the table, silent in the room loud with a ticking clock, and at last I released the shuddering breath I had locked up in my chest.

"The farm," I said softly, "is mine. My pa bought and paid for it three years ago, when first we came. He's dead—they're all dead—and the farm comes to me. *You* know that." I swallowed heavily, feeling an odd lightheadedness as I stared at him. I nearly laughed at the absurdity of it all. How could he tell me the farm wasn't mine?

"Lonnie—"

"No," I interrupted. "You know all of this. You stood by me from the very first when the bank wished to sell it away from me. When they foolishly thought I had people to go home to in Ohio." I smiled at him. "Only I didn't. And you spoke against the bank on my behalf."

He nodded. "I believed you had a clear claim. Then."

"Then!" I stared at him, aghast. "How can you believe otherwise? I *do* have a clear claim. This place is mine."

"Lonnie," he said with endless patience, "you must understand about deeds and liens, and payments. The bank has gone over the records, and they've found something that may mean the farm isn't yours at all."

"I don't care about deeds and liens, or whatever else the bank might have concocted to bother me. All I know is my pa paid good money for this place, and it's mine. No one—not even you—says differently."

He was saddened and suddenly weary. I realized abruptly he had no more stomach for this than I had.

"I know. This is an ugly business. A man from the bank came to me and said—knowing I knew you best—that you were about to lose the place. I said I'd better come instead." He smiled ruefully. "Knowing your stubbornness and pride, I thought it best if I brought the news. I thought you might set Tracker on the man."

"I would've," I said firmly, then shook my head in disbelief. "What does this mean? How can the bank say such a thing? Pa paid for it!"

Barton rubbed at his thinning hair, still upset by

circumstances. "There was some kind of mix-up in the records. You pa paid Mr. Owen, the original owner, for the land, but Owen never completed his own payments to the bank. Don't you see? The deed wasn't clear to begin with. Mr. Owen never had the right to sell the way he did."

I felt horribly hollow inside. "It was bought in good faith."

"Lonnie . . ."

I stared at him, desolated. "How could it take them *this long?*"

"Small-town banks keep a lot of records for people on neighboring farms. Someone called for an audit to make certain things were right, and they turned up the record on the farm. But there still might be a chance. They haven't completed a second check, and maybe things will turn up differently."

I stared down at the table, not really seeing the worn wood or my clenched hands resting on it rigidly. "What happens if they find the claim ain't clear?"

"The farm reverts to the bank. It becomes their property."

My belly lurched. "What would they do with it?"

He looked grim and sounded worse. "Sell it. Like they intended to in the first place. They get no profit so long as the place is yours, Lonnie. Only if they can sell it to someone else."

I felt washed out, useless. Old and infirm. "What can I do? What can I do to clear the deed?"

Barton reached across the table and put his big hand over both of mine, holding them firmly to give me strength. I had always liked him, but even from him it was bitter, horrid news.

"You can do nothing, Lonnie."

I felt bloodless, staring at him helplessly. "Nothing?"

"Unless, somehow, you could pay off what's left on the debt. Can you do that?"

I bit my lip in response to his gentle tone. All I could do was whisper to him. "No. You know I can't."

"Lonnie, you're a proud girl. I know what this is doing to you. But Emily and I would love to have you come stay with us." He sounded strangely wistful. "Since she lost the last baby the doctor says there will be no more. We've always had our hearts set on a girl."

"You've got three fine boys. And I've done all of my growing. It's not like I could be a baby to you both."

He smiled painfully. "I know that. But I also know how you feel, how settled your mind is on what you want to do. You still have a home, Lonnie, always. With us."

He was only trying to be kind, and I knew it, but bitterness welled up in me with such force all I could do was stare speechlessly at him. The farm was sliding out of my hands into the greedy grasp of bankers who wanted a profit, caring little for the people they might force out of a home. I couldn't find it in my soul to speak decent to the man who came for the bank, even though the man was Abner Barton. I lifted my head stiffly and set my eyes to his, withdrawing my hands from under his callused palm.

"They'll have to burn me out before they get me off my land."

"Lonnie—"

"Tell them that. Tell them that's gospel from Lonnie Ryan."

He shook his head slowly, like a wounded bull. Pain filled his eyes, pain I'd put there. But I couldn't wish it back.

"Lonnie, I know this sounds harsh to you. I'm sorry I had to bring you this news. But I thought it was better from a friend than a stranger."

"I'd expect such news from a stranger. Never from you."

He cleared his throat. "I had a lot of respect for you pa, Lonnie. He was a good man, a strong man, someone who saw this land for what it might be someday. I didn't get the chance to know him long, but I knew him as a fair-minded man who did things right. Lonnie, I'd hate to see you butting heads against the legal ways. He raised you too well for that."

My jaw clenched. "He raised me to be proud, Mr. Barton, and to stand up for what's right. To stand *against* whatever's wrong. He would not allow his land to be lost to a money-minded banker, and he would not allow me to lose it. There's an end to it."

He drew in a deep breath, defeat in his eyes. "I'm only warning you. If the bank finds in its own favor, which is very likely, you'll have no more right to stay here. You'll be a squatter."

The insult hit home with all the impact the loaded word carried with it. It sent a shudder of anger and pain through my bones and brought rage flushing to

98

my face. I got to my feet. My face was set so hard it hurt.

"A Ryan is not a squatter. The land is paid for. This debt Mr. Owen needs to pay has nothing to do with my family, or what's left of it." I tried to smile, but it came out like a wolf's snarl. "You tell the bank that, Mr. Barton, tell them from me. I've been called names before. I don't guess this one will hurt me."

He rose slowly. We faced one another across the table. He had my unspoken leave to go, so he walked to the door and stepped out. I followed him and picked up the rifle leaning by the door.

Barton gathered his reins and mounted the sorrel gelding. Horse and rider loomed a shadow across the yard as he looked down at me. His face had aged and his blue eyes were sick and saddened, and also resigned.

"Lonnie, I've got to admit you've got grit. I never expected you to take kindly to my words." He sighed heavily and began to smile. "I think the bank may find it has a powerful enemy in you, my girl. And I want you to know—I'll back you up."

I said nothing as he wheeled his horse and put it to a lope heading up the hill to the road. He was a good man to call friend and I knew it had hurt him to bring me the message. At least I had one man on my side.

I stared after him with the rifle clenched in my arms as if I'd lose it if I let go. Tracker nosed at me and I dropped a hand down, brushing the flea-bitten ears.

Now they wanted my land.

"Lonnie."

It was Toby in the doorway, three steps behind. I

didn't bother to turn, but heaved a sigh heavy enough to lift my shoulders and drop them.

"Lonnie, I heard what he said."

"It would be hard not to," I said bitterly, "seeing as how you were just in the other room."

He walked out and stood beside me, silent. I turned my head and met his eyes.

There was a strange look in them. He, who loved to prod me into a fight with words, looked at me as if he understood. But I was past caring what he thought. I had more important things on my mind.

Dan Michael Loggins came out of the house and grasped my shoulder in one of his big hands, turning me to face them both.

"What will you do now, my girl?" he asked.

"Just what I said."

"You'll fight them?" asked Toby quietly.

"With everything I've got."

Loggins smiled crookedly beneath his mustache. "They'll win, you know. You don't stand a chance. You're only a girl, and half-grown at that. How could you possibly stand against them?"

I shook my head and smiled. "That is something I've heard before. From you, and Toby, and all the others in town." I turned away from them and started walking toward the cornfield.

Toby called after me. "Lonnie—it's a *bank*. It's got powerful men running it. How can one lone girl stand against men with money?"

"I'm not alone!"

"Who've you got *with* you?"

I halted at the crest of the hill. I stood against the sunlight, feeling its warmth on my face. Tracker was at my side, and I hefted the rifle in one hand.

"I've got my dog and a gun. What more do I need?"

"Lonnie!" His voice was incredulous. "It's only land!"

My fingers clenched on the rifle. "And it's *mine*."

He stared at me as I turned and started up the next rise. "Lonnie—where are you going?"

I smiled in secret solitude, oddly content after hearing such bad news. I was strangely secure in what I had called down to him.

I knew as long as I had Tracker and my gun, nothing could take my land from me.

PART II

"The Barstows"

Chapter Six

Abner Barton's visit soured me. Suddenly I drew back into my shell, the one I'd carefully constructed to keep my sanity when first I set out to make a living, and I needed it again. Badly. Something in me had loosened since Toby and Loggins had come along; I'd become affable and talkative, something I'd never dealt with before. I recognized the change in me, and realized I'd have to do something about it. If I was to survive, I couldn't let anyone get close to me.

Dan Michael Loggins, with his quiet looks at me and gentle smiles, knew exactly what I did. But he said nothing. Perhaps he realized I needed the time to myself to rebuild my shell so I could keep them all out. But I was grateful for his silence.

But Toby was different. He took it on himself as a personal challenge to drag me back into his world, and he made it difficult. The man was a wizard with words, twisting me up one side and down the other with some of the odd discussions we got into. Loggins watched us like a paternal presence, and I resented that, too.

"You have no sense of humor," Toby announced

one morning as we sat over breakfast.

I stared at him across the rim of my mug. "Do you really think this situation calls for one?"

"Certainly it does. It's not as bad as it could be." He scooped up a dab of jam with a biscuit. "After all, no one from the bank has been by to make you leave."

"They'd best not come, either."

He grinned lazily at me. "Tell me, would you shoot them?"

I grinned, but it was more a baring of fangs. "I most certainly would."

Loggins finished up his meal. "Do you think it's so easy, then?"

Toby and I both stared at him, caught by an odd note in his quiet tone. I opened my mouth to insist that I was completely capable of shooting, then thought better of it. Hunting was one thing, but could I shoot a man? Could I willingly take another's life?

I saw the gleam in Loggins' green eyes and realized what he did. Abruptly it made me angry. "You've said you've got little faith in me, bounty hunter, you've made that plain enough. But I'll do whatever I have to. It's my land and I'll keep it."

"I only asked if you honestly thought you could kill a man."

Toby's brows rose as he considered the problem, but I just stared Loggins down. "You'll not get me to say flat out what I will and will not do. I can't know for certain. But I'd say there's a good bet I just might be able to shoot a man. Should he bring me trouble."

Toby scratched at his jaw. "Dan Michael—have you shot a man?"

He set down his fork and drew his pipe from a pocket. Carefully he began to pack it, then lit it and waited until it was going to his satisfaction. The production irritated me for some reason, and I realized he was stalling. Or else he wanted to make certain we were listening.

"Children," he said softly, purposefully, "I've killed more than one. I was fortunate to have it within the bounds of the law, for I did it as sheriff." His eyes were hard as he looked at each of us. "But it made it no easier. Killing a man is harsh work, no matter how easy the bullet flies from the gun." He puffed on the pipe a moment, then withdrew it and fixed me with a piercing stare. "Do you understand that, Lonnie?"

I swallowed. "I think I do, Mr. Loggins."

He smiled, then nodded and rose. "Children, it's time I left."

"Left!" Toby exclaimed. "You're leaving?"

"I must. I've spent too long here as it is." He grinned at me. "And I think I've been a burden on Lonnie's spirit."

I wanted to protest, but realized it might display the fact I held some emotion for the man. It was not in me to let him know I cared, just a little. I just met his smile and inclined my head.

"It's purely been a pleasure, Dan Michael Loggins."

He grinned again at the irony in my tone, and nodded in my direction. "My compliments to the lady of the house. She's been an excellent host."

"I wish you'd stay," Toby said.

Loggins moved around the room, gathering up his

107

belongings. He packed them all into his saddlebags and sighed, meeting Toby's eyes.

"Toby, my young friend, I've overstayed my welcome. Though I never really got one." He shot me an amused glance. "And it's time I left. But you should know something, my friend."

"What?"

"She'll be asking *you* to leave soon enough, as well."

"Me?"

Loggins pointed at him with the pipe. "You're only a temporary guest, you know, brought about by strange circumstances. You're nearly healed. She'll have you on your way before you know it."

Toby glanced back at me with strangeness in his eyes. Then he laughed, and looked back at Loggins. "So she will. I'd near forgotten why I was here."

The mustache twisted in a smile. "I know. But you'd best remember, before you lose more of yourself."

Toby stared at him, uncomprehending, and I lifted my head as Loggins' words seeped in. I thought I knew his intent, and I didn't like it.

"I need no help from either of you," I said calmly.

"I reckon not," Loggins remarked, and walked softly from the house.

Toby went with him for his goodbye, but I stayed in the house and thought on the man's odd words. He was saying more than what was heard, and I was afraid to decipher the meaning. But I had a feeling I knew.

"Toby must go," I said softly to myself. "Before I

108

learn to depend on a man who is totally undependable."

He was a puzzle to me, more so than I to him. Deep down I believed he understood how much I cared about my land, though he scoffed, himself, and treated the subject lightly. Once I'd asked him again how he could desert his family like he had, but he cut me short by saying he wanted his freedom.

"Don't you ever want to put down roots?" I had asked.

He shrugged as he sat in the rocker with Patch in his lap and Tracker at his feet. "It's not that I don't want to put down roots. It's that I want to choose the proper place and time."

"But what about an inheritance? The dairy's partly yours."

"No, the place is going to my brothers. My father ruled me out of my inheritance when I butted heads with him over working."

"See there?" I told him. "That's what happens when you go against something that's been right for so long."

He shook his head, exasperated. "The dairy never meant the same to me. Why should I care if he leaves it to my brothers? I didn't even get along with *them*."

"Seems to me you don't get along with much of anybody."

He laughed aloud and shook his head. "I get along with you just fine!"

"You don't get along with me. I tolerate you. There's a world of difference."

"Is there?"

"Course there is. You're a wounded man I'm tending to. No more."

"Tell me, Lonnie, would you want more?"

I averted my eyes and smoothed the wrinkles from my faded dress. "There is no more, Toby. You'll be gone when you're healed. Soon enough, now."

An odd expression crossed his face and he abruptly changed the subject. "Had your family not been killed, what do you think you'd be doing right now?"

I chewed at my lip, thinking deeply. It seemed strange to consider a thing so far removed from what I was, but I eventually came to an answer.

"Maybe I'd be married off," I said. "Maybe I'd even have a baby." I hunched a shoulder. "All that got changed."

"So did you, I think."

"Well, if I did it's because I had to. And it ain't so bad."

"Isn't. And I can't help but think once you were like every other girl. Laughing and playing, and thinking easier of people."

I stiffened. "You're saying I'm bitter and harsh?"

"A little," he said softly.

The flush came hot to my face and even stung my eyes. What he said didn't hurt that much, not really, but what surprised me was that it hurt at all.

Somehow he'd found a crack in my wall, and I had to rebuild it. One way of doing that was to tear down some of his. I sat stiffly on the rug and held his curious eyes.

"I'd like to see *you* try it. I'd like to see you *try* to do what I've done. You rate your life by freedom. You say it's all right to follow a dream. But it don't put

110

food in your mouth." I sucked in a painful breath as he stared at me, stricken by my lashing tone of constrained anger. "I may be bitter and harsh at seventeen, but it's because I had to grow up fast. Losing my daydreams is the price I've had to pay."

"Lonnie, I only meant—"

"I know what you meant!" The venom in my voice struck through his attempt at placation. "But haven't you found that dreams don't always work? You saw men getting murdered, Toby. Try dreaming yourself out of the trouble you're in." I swallowed and held his startled eyes. "Or ain't a Barstow bullet proof enough that life *can* be bitter and harsh?"

His face drained of color and his knuckles were bone-white as he gripped the rocker arms with all his strength. He was undergoing his own inner battle, I saw, and I wondered which side would win. I wanted a fight, something we could both scream and rage about, and I hoped he'd oblige me.

Instead, suddenly, he surrendered the battle. "All right. I'll concede most of what you said. But there's one thing you're very wrong about."

I laughed shortly. "What's that?"

He smiled grimly. "That I couldn't do what you've done."

"You! You turned your back on your family. You'd never last a day out here with real work on your hands. You'd run from it, like before."

The scorn in my voice brought color blazing to his face and drove him to his feet. The rocker creaked and swung back from the movement, and Patch flew from his lap to escape the violent motion. His fists clenched.

111

"I could do it! If I had your pride and determination, I'd do it in a second!"

Silence fell between us like a heavy curtain. I stared up at him with my mouth foolishly open, and even after I closed it the wonder of his fury still reeled in my brain. But I couldn't let it rest. I had to know what he meant.

"It seems to me," I said, picking my way carefully, "that you truly do understand what I am and what I'm doing out here by myself."

"Of course I understand what you're doing. Just because I don't happen to share this obsession you have for your land doesn't mean I can't comprehend it."

I was stunned. "Then why have you fussed at me about it? Why do you tell me I'm foolish to care so much?"

Suddenly his grin was back, and with it came the teasing glint in his eyes. "I only wanted to hear what you'd say. I wanted to see how far you'd go. Now I know you mean exactly what you say."

I glared up at him. "I don't make a habit of lying."

"Lying has nothing to do with it. Females say a lot of things they never mean. But you're not like most females."

I laughed hollowly. "No, I'm surely not. You said I was bitter and harsh."

"So you are, but you defended yourself admirably."

I brushed back loose hair, fighting down the sudden pain in my chest. "Against the truth? It's a hollow victory."

Toby knelt down before me, smiling gently. "With

112

any less prickly, quick pride you'd never last a day out here. You're what you are because you have to be. I can't fight that." He put a hand out and lifted my chin. "And I don't want to."

Abruptly things turned inside out. I couldn't tell daylight from the darkness, and Toby had made it that way. I knew he'd done it purposely, to confuse me within my mind, and he had succeeded. I drew away from his hand and rose, walking to the open doorway. Loggins was at the well, drawing up a bucket of water.

"Lonnie," Toby said quietly.

I closed my eyes, trying to ignore him. Maybe if I said nothing he'd give it up.

He didn't. "Lonnie?"

I sighed and felt it tremble. "What now, Toby?"

"Forget what I said. I didn't mean it."

I smiled sadly out into the yard. "I didn't figure you did."

Now I sat in the rocker as he came back in the house from saying his last words to Loggins. I came out of my recollections and watched him silently, noting the concern in his face. He glanced up and saw me watching him, and smiled.

"He's right. I've gotten used to being here. I'd near forgotten you'll send me on my way."

"You can't stay here forever."

"No, I guess I can't." He sat down on the rug and folded his legs beneath him, taking Tracker's head in his hands so he could wool at the hound's ears.

"Lonnie, do you really think you could shoot someone?"

"I gave Loggins my answer."

113

"Tell *me*."

"I'd do what needs doing."

"Even if it means taking another man's life?"

"It would all depend on the man. Some men deserve killing."

"Like the Barstow gang?"

So that was it. I smiled. "Kansas would be better off without them."

"Well, I don't know if I could ever shoot anyone."

"You can't know until it happens."

He stared grimly down at Tracker. "No, I reckon not."

I began to rock the chair slowly, feeling some of what was bothering him. But I didn't want him to think about it. He was nearly healed and his strength was coming back, but sickness hung on if the mind was uneasy.

"Toby, don't even think about the Barstow gang. Loggins left. It means they likely won't come. Not yet. Maybe never."

He pushed Tracker's head from his lap and rose. "I just can't forget about it."

I said nothing and watched him walk out the door.

"So," I said softly when he'd left, "you really do care. Deep down in your drifter's soul, you really do care."

I found him at the lean-to, inspecting Princess and her bulging sides. He knew milk cows, all right, he handled her simply and effectively without a second thought. The cow stayed calm even with strange hands on her, but the brown mare eyed him closely, edgily.

I'd come up on him quietly, but Tory knew I was there. "Your cow ought to calve in a week or two."

"I'm hoping for a heifer."

"And if it's a bull-calf?"

"I'll sell it back to the farmer with the breeding bull. Princess is a good cow."

"She's all you have left?"

I knew what he meant. "I have the mare, too, and the chickens. It's hard to run chickens off very far."

He smiled. "I guess so. I never thought about it."

He slid a glance over the mare, marking the white gall spots. It was obvious she was nothing more than a work animal now, and equally obvious once she'd been more.

Toby turned away and stared out across the land. He was oddly restless about something. Finally he rolled his shoulders in a half-shrug and looked at me.

"Let's go look at your precious land."

I raised my eyebrows. "Starting where?"

"The river. I need a bath."

I grinned. "I thought you'd never see that. Well, follow me."

First he wanted only to look, so I obliged by escorting him down to the river. I led him to the cool shaded pool where I did my bathing. Toby stopped at the river bank, but I toed my way out on the felled cottonwood that extended into the water. Patch chased a butterfly and Tracker went into the shallows, lapping at the water.

"It's pretty," Toby said.

"It's my favorite spot. This is where I was coming from the day I found you."

"I've never thanked you properly for that."

I shrugged, balancing carefully. "No need. It had

115

to be done."

"You should hang a rope from that big tree. It would make a good swing."

"I haven't got time to swing."

I stood out over the river, safe on the huge trunk, peering contentedly across the far bank. I felt lighthearted and filled with goodwill, but when Toby stepped up beside me I stiffened.

"What are you doing?"

"I intend to thank you properly. And I've got you in just the spot for it. You can't get away."

I looked at him over my shoulder. "Why? What do you have planned that might drive me to flight?"

He grasped my shoulders and turned me before I could speak. I started to protest, but his mouth came down on mine and words were useless. I grabbed at him only to keep myself upright, for my feet slid on the gnarled trunk, but he seemed to think I meant more by it. Suddenly panicking, I shoved at him and only succeeded in wrenching myself off balance. I was the one who went in the river. Not him.

I swam up to the surface, furious. He stood safely upon the trunk clutching his belly, laughing hysterically. I sucked in air and caught my breath, chilled, standing up in the waist-deep water.

"You!" I sputtered helplessly. "You are a monster!"

The bank, as I crawled out, was slimy with mud. I fell back once, covered with the muck, and ducked down in the water to wash it off. Tracker splashed happily about trying to save me, but I shoved him away and told him crossly to get out of the water before he drowned me.

Toby came over and reached down to me, bracing himself on the bank. "Come on, I'll get you out."

"You're the one who got me *in!*"

"You fell, and you know it. If you'd stood quietly you'd never have fallen in."

"Toby Markham, you're despicable!"

His eyebrows lanced up. "I didn't know you knew such words existed."

With what dignity I could muster I squeezed water out of my braid and glared wrathfully up at him. "My ma was an educated woman. Of course I know such words."

"Come on."

His grasp was sure and strong as he caught me by the wrist and hauled me out of the water. I nearly slipped again and he caught me around the waist, pulling me close to steady me. I tried to pull away, but he held me firmly.

"Let go. Haven't you 'thanked' me enough?"

"Lonnie—"

"Let me go."

He did finally. I slicked water off my face and started to walk away, conscious of my soaked state. Toby caught up and walked along with me.

"Haven't you ever been kissed before?"

I blushed fiery red.

"Oh. So you *have.*"

I slid him a furious look. "At a dance," I said grudgingly. "In town. My fifteenth birthday."

"It's a good birthday present."

I wrung out my braid again. "There wasn't any need for it then, and there certainly ain't now."

He laughed softly. "I'm sorry, I didn't mean to

upset you."

"I expect I'll survive."

"No one's kissed you since then?"

I looked at him in disgust. "Who is there? The cow? I'm not exactly crawling with beaux out here, you know."

"No," he said thoughtfully. "I guess you're not."

"Which is what I prefer."

"So you said. Lonnie, I didn't push you in."

"It's true you didn't push," I admitted, scowling. "But you helped."

"Are you angry I laughed?"

I heaved a long-suffering sigh. "No, I'm not angry you laughed."

"Good."

"Why 'good'?"

"Because it was funny."

Chapter Seven

I changed into dry clothes and undid my braid, combing it out as I walked back into the front room. Toby stood there with a ball of brown soap and a rough towel in his hands.

I held up a delaying hand. "Wait. You've been wearing that old shirt of Dan Michael's for long enough. I've got something better for you."

In the bedroom I dug into the trunk still holding my pa's clothing, and found a gray linsey shirt. After a momentary pang of recollection I handed it over to Toby.

"Your father's?"

"It ain't mine."

"Isn't." He smiled. "Thanks, Lonnie."

I braided my hair, wondering why he watched me so intently. I chewed at my lip a moment, then spoke. "I won't be here when you come back."

"Where will you be?"

"In town. I need supplies."

"Is that all?" he demanded, watching me with knowing eyes. His tone stung at me.

"What else would I be doing?"

"Don't you mean you'll be stopping at the bank to argue about the farm?"

I felt color flood my face as I clenched my jaw. "I'll just tell them flat out what I feel. That's not arguing."

He laughed. "No, it isn't. An argument takes two people, and you're too stubborn to hear anybody else out."

I walked straight past him and got all the way outside before I dredged up a good reply. Once I had it I stopped and turned, facing him as he stood framed in the doorway.

"I'm not at all surprised the Barstows are hunting you down. You'd make anybody mad."

His eyes were bright and his teeth shone in a grin. "Do I make you mad, Lonnie?"

"No." I smiled back at him, triumphant. "You have to care about someone in order to get mad. I don't care about you at all."

I went off to the lean-to to harness the mare to the buckboard; his laughter followed me all the way.

I hitched her up, gathered all my tradeable goods and a small part of my cash hoard, which God knew wasn't much, and climbed up to tuck the rifle beneath the seat. I whistled Tracker into the buckboard and gathered up the reins, clucking to the mare.

She started out smartly, glad of the exercise, and I lost myself in the day. The mare knew the way to town as well as I did, so I sat idle on the seat, hardly reining her at all. I was lulled by the sun's warmth, luxuriating in the peaceful sensation as we crossed the prairie plains.

As the buckboard drew closer to town I looked at Ridgely with new eyes, recalling what I'd told Toby of the place. In addition to the two saloons there was Barton's livery, Tolleson's dry goods store, Larsson's grocery, the bank, and a dress goods shop. At the close end of town stood a little white church. As if to mock it, a nearly identical building stood at the other end of town, somehow separated from Ridgely.

Three ladies lived in the little white house, though no one else would have been decent enough to call them that. The farmwomen and town wives avoided looking at the place, but there was little enough reason for them to do it.

The ladies of the house were seen in both saloons with great regularity, sometimes the dress goods shop and the grocery, and very rarely in church. Mostly they kept themselves out of sight.

I couldn't figure out why they'd count Ridgely as a good place to settle, even for a short space. But I guess their sort of lives didn't leave them much room for choice. The men stayed away from their house during the day, but nighttime brought another story.

Several times on my trips in I had met up with one of the ladies unexpectedly, and she always smiled and said a pleasant word or two. I guess in some strange fashion she knew the folks in town looked on me differently too. But there all likeness ended. She wasn't much taller than me and her brown hair was piled on top of her head. She wore a high-necked, long-sleeved dress when shopping. The gold tooth in the front of her mouth gleamed whenever she laughed or smiled. She laughed a lot. I wondered if it was by nature or for the tooth.

I passed the saloons which, oddly, stood directly across the street from one another. I always wondered if they had been placed that way purposely, as if a drunk might stumble out of one saloon right into the other.

The farmers, I knew, visited the saloons mostly on Saturday nights. Then they went to church the next morning to atone for their sinning.

I passed Barton's smithy and Elmer Tolleson's feed store, then halted the mare before Olaf Larsson's grocery. I tied her to the hitch rail and went in to see the Swede.

He was a tall, thin man who wore gold-rimmed spectacles. His hair had grayed years before, taking the rest of his color with it, and his thin shoulders were slightly stooped. His words were always kind and his nature better still, belying the years of loneliness come upon him after the deaths of his wife and son.

He glanced up as I entered, ringing the little silver bell he'd hung on the handle. He was carefully measuring sugar into ten- and twenty-pound bags, but he took time away from his ladling to nod at me and speak. I loved to hear his accent and the curious cadence of his talk.

"Lonnie, you got things to trade me today?"

"The usual, and some sausages."

"Bring them in, then, please. We will do business like usual, you and I."

I unloaded my trade goods and took them back into the store, setting each item carefully on the counter. Two other customers came in as I unloaded, and I stepped back to let them go first. I always felt self-conscious when faced with townsfolk, for no one ever let me forget I'd acted strangely after the murders.

But the Swede wouldn't let me fade into the background. "If you ladies will wait only a moment, please, I will help Lonnie with her business."

I couldn't miss the affronted looks I received from the two women, but ignored them. Finally Larsson nodded and peered over his spectacle rims at me.

"You have good things, Lonnie, like always. Give me your list, and I will give you what else you got coming."

I fished the paper out of a pocket and handed it across. He studied it, shoving at his glasses, and nodded.

"This will do. You have enough goods to cover what you want. I'll gather them up and put them in your wagon."

I nodded. "Thank you. I'll come back for them later."

Outside on the boardwalk I stared down the street until I found the bank. Slowly I walked to it and paused, staring at the tall false front. The building sported two glass windows, but I couldn't see in because the sunshades were drawn down. Thoughtfully I read the gold scrolly letters painted across the windows:

RIDGELY BANK
MACKLIN COUNTY, KANSAS
We keep your money and your trust safe

I was not impressed. They hadn't one penny of my money, and they surely didn't have an ounce of my trust. Certainly not when they were happily willing to pitch me off my land just to make a profit.

Smiling evilly to myself, I put a hand to the door and went in.

For all the fancy writing on the window and the tall false front, it wasn't terribly big inside. The front room was small, divided in half by a counter like a saloon had, only this one held up little barred windows. One man sat behind the divider. The place was empty so he was forced to look at me, peering through the little cage.

"Can I help you, miss?"

"My name is Lonnie Ryan," I said flatly. "I've come to see the man that wants my land."

He blinked. I could tell immediately he wasn't the one I was after, not this bald-headed, puffy-faced man. He was a worker, not an owner.

"I beg your pardon?" he said insultingly.

I went forward and faced him through his little cage. "You heard me quite well. I intend to see the man who wants my land." I stared him down. "Who's the one responsible for deeds?"

He sniffed. "You mean Mr. Higgins. He's the *president* of this bank."

"I want the owner. The one who handles all the papers and records."

His tiny smile was openly mocking and his manner condescending. "Mr. Higgins *is* the man who handles all legal matters involved with land claims, deeds and so forth."

"Then I'll see him. Where's he hiding?"

He flushed brick-red and gestured to a door behind him. "The president's office is through there. Shall I make an appointment for you?"

I glared back at him, fed up. "I don't need an appointment. He'll see me without one. The greedy banker wants my farm."

That shocked him to his shoes. His puffy face flushed again and the loose muscles in his neck trembled. I kept my eyes flat with his and marched around the divider, through the door, and into the president's office.

Higgins was seated at a big desk, reared back in his chair to show off the gold watch chain glinting across the expanse of his vested belly. He wore a dark suit with starched linen shirt, and his gray hair was slicked back smooth from his forehead. His yellowish eyes were startled as I came in without a by-your-leave, then went instantly shrewd. I knew right away he wasn't a man to fool with.

"Mr. Polt normally shows visitors in, miss. May I ask your business?"

His voice was heavy and rich. He wasn't at all impressed with me; I wasn't the impressive sort. I summoned up my strength and put it in my voice.

"I'm here on a land matter, mister. Something I want settled now."

His eyes glimmered faintly as he recognized the brassy defiance in my tone. He inclined his head slightly and made a smooth gesture toward a chair before the desk.

"Please be seated. I'm sure this matter can be settled without difficulty."

I hesitated, then angrily sat down as he'd bid. I tried to look calm as I perched on the chair, and though I was sure of my position, I couldn't help but feel ill-at-ease. I didn't think blustering defiance would mean much to banker Higgins, who was likely very used to it.

The wooden slats of the chair dug into my back as I slid into it, so I pushed forward again and remained perched. I was horribly conscious of my faded clothes and bare feet. I folded my sunburned, callused hands in my lap.

Higgins leaned forward in his chair and steepled his fingers, resting his hands on the desk. "Which land are you here about?"

"The Ryan farm by the river. I mean to tell you it's my land and you have no claim to it. It came to me on my pa's death."

"You're Lonnie. Lonnie Ryan."

"I am."

Oddly, he smiled. He seemed to take my measure for a long moment, then nodded. He raised an illustrative index finger.

"Your father owed the bank payments on that land when he died."

"My father owed nothing. It was Mr. Owen who failed to pay. It's his debt, not my pa's or mine."

He wasn't smiling any longer. "Mr. Owen has long since left Ridgely. That makes your father liable. Now you, of course, since he's dead."

"Didn't Abner Barton come to see you?"

His smile was completely gone now. "He came and gave me a message he said was from you. So, you mean to fight the bank."

"I'll fight you, Mr. Higgins. You appear to be the bank."

"If we find in our favor, our claim to the land is

126

entirely legal."

I shrugged. "Legal or not, the land's staying mine. You'll have to burn me out to get me off my land." I smiled grimly. "And then what would your precious claim be worth?"

He looked stunned at the magnitude of my assurance, and I didn't waste time letting him come up with a reply. I got up and walked to the door. There I paused.

"The land is mine," I said softly, "and I mean to keep it however I can."

I found Abner Barton sweating at his anvil, pounding out a red-hot iron horse shoe. The double doors of the big livery were open to encourage any wandering breeze, but it was scorching by the coals. It was the sort of heat that smelled, biting at the lungs. I watched the massive hammer falling in a ringing rhythm of blows, each one curving the hot metal a little closer to the proper shape. I loved to see the magic done.

A roan horse was tied near, awaiting a new shoe. Barton nodded and smiled at me in welcome, but didn't stop so the shoe wouldn't cool too quickly. I gestured at the roan.

"Whose horse?"

"Stranger's. Rode in earlier."

I tried not to wince each time the hammer struck iron. It always took me a moment to accustom myself to the clangor.

"Any news?" I asked idly, knowing part of a smith's payment was in stories from his customers.

Abner Barton flashed me a queer sideways look and his eyes veiled abruptly. The suddenness of it startled me.

"Mr. Barton—"

"Nothing, Lonnie. He told me nothing."

A prickle of foreboding ran up my spine. Silently I watched as he pushed the shoe beneath the coals to heat again, and he wiped away the sweat on his brow with an impatient gesture. His eyes were blank as he met mine.

"What is it?" I asked. "What is it you're not telling me?"

He sighed and sat down on a bench by the doors. "I'd like it if you came to stay with Emily and me for a few days."

"I'm not leaving my land, no matter what the bank says."

He gestured sharply. "This has nothing to do with the bank. It's something entirely different." He met my eyes squarely. "There's trouble on the way. Matt Barstow and his boys are headed this way. I'd rather you came to stay with us while there's a chance men like them are on the prowl."

"The Barstows," I said blankly, staring at the glowing coals. I sucked in a quick breath and tried to sound innocently curious. "Why would they be coming here?"

Barton brushed at his damp brow. "Some story of a man who testified against Ben Barstow and got him hanged. Matt and the others are looking for him, to render their own sort of justice, I expect." He shook his head. "The Barstows are bad enough just robbing. Something like this, well, I doubt much'll

128

stop them."

"That witness wouldn't stand much of a chance, then, would he? If they caught him?"

Barton coughed and spat. "I'd not give you a penny for his chances. I hope he's hiding out somewhere. Somewhere safe."

"So do I," I said fervently.

"So," he said, rising to return to his work, "will you be coming?"

I stared into his guileless eyes and reflected again how fortunate I was to have such a man to call a friend. For all my high-handed insistence of doing on my own, I'd had help. I smiled at him crookedly and shook my head.

"You know I can't. I appreciate the offer, for I know you made it for my own good, but I'll risk the trouble. I don't dare leave the farm right now, and let the bank get its claws into it."

"Lonnie, I want you safe."

"I know that. I will be. You'll see."

Before he could protest any more I said a fast farewell and went back to Larsson's store. He'd loaded my buckboard and I looked over my supplies: flour, grain, chicken feed, salt, sugar and canned goods. I went in and thanked the Swede, then clambered up onto the buckboard and lifted the reins to go.

Before I could, Tracker fell over the seat to greet me with a couple of tongue-swipes, and I had to thank him and shove him off me. As I did so I heard two men approaching, talking excitedly, so I gave in to curiosity and listened.

"Barstow's mad enough to spit nails over his

brother's hanging."

The other man shrugged. "I reckon even outlaws get riled over blood kin's death."

"But the man in the saloon said him and his gang are comin' here."

The second man snorted. "Here? What would Barstows want with us? We're little more than a waterin' hole."

"I heard the witness who got Ben hanged might be hereabouts."

"Aw, Charlie, you put too much stock in what you hear. Liquor lies. Tells tales."

Then they were gone. A chill sprang up in my bones. Liquor lied and it told tall tales, but I knew a speck of truth often started such cheap saloon talk. Barstow news was common news, passed around eagerly with flourishes added at every telling. But this time it hit home with a vengeance, and I felt apprehension wash through me with a lash of quick fear.

I unloaded the supplies at the storage shed by the lean-to. Tracker ran off to the river and a moment later I heard his ringing bell. But it wasn't trouble he meant, so I let him be.

I led the mare to the well and cranked up the bucket slowly, letting her cool before she drank. The trip to Ridgely wasn't terribly hard on her, for the buckboard was light even when loaded, but I couldn't risk wearing her out. I'd never be able to afford another horse.

She pushed at me, shoving insistently for the

water, so I set the bucket within reach and held it steady. She plunged her muzzle in and sucked up the liquid, nearly upsetting the bucket. I chastised her for it and she lifted her streaming muzzle and snorted water all over me. I think she did it purposely.

It was as I carried the last of the supplies into the house that I first sensed the wrongness. I couldn't put a name to it, but it came clearly to my senses. I halted in the middle of the room and looked around, frowning, trying to understand the prickly feeling in my bones.

Abruptly I knew what it was. I missed something. Something wasn't right.

Toby was gone.

He wasn't at the river. Next I climbed the rise to the cottonwood tree by the cornfield and stood there, peering across the land. All I saw were birds wheeling against the sky.

I thought perhaps he'd wandered along the river bank after his bath, so I went back there. As I hurried along I realized I was behaving as if I cared.

That stopped me a moment, just long enough to realize I'd finally admitted it to myself. All the staunch denials I'd made had been wrenched away from me.

I cared for Toby, all right. A sight more than I knew.

I clutched the rifle to me and wandered through the deep grass by the sluggish river. At a curve I finally halted, quitting my search to stare blankly into the water. I conjured up the idea that somehow the Barstows had found him but, sadly, I knew better than that. I turned and walked slowly back to the house, acknowledging the horrible heavy feeling threading its painful way through my bones.

Tracker whined deep in his throat as I set the rifle on its pegs. For a moment I stood gazing into his mournful hound eyes, then shook my head and sighed.

"You knew, didn't you? You knew he was gone the minute we got back." I smiled down at his beloved face. "Ah, Tracker, if only I had your sense."

I sat down in the rocker. I was horribly empty. Toby had left without a word of thanks.

Grimly I realized it wasn't the thanks I missed. It was the goodbye.

Chapter Eight

Princess yanked me from my reverie. Her bawling came to me from the lean-to with imperativeness, and I answered. When I got to her she was down on her side, breathing fast and heavy. I untied the brown mare and took her around back of the storage shed, tying her there so she wouldn't bother Princess.

The cow was very restless, turning her head to peer at her hindquarters, bawling plaintively. I knelt at her side, stroking her heaving flanks. I tried to calm her with soft speech, but it didn't work. I knew something was wrong, though I was no expert at calving.

"Lonnie, I'll help the cow."

I jerked upright, stunned by Toby's voice. He looked back at me silently, a whole world held in his eyes, then dropped the burlap bag he carried and moved in next to me.

"Mix up a warm grain mash for her. She'll need it when she's through."

"You know about this?" I asked, glad to have a safe subject to converse about.

He laughed, but there wasn't much humor in it. "I'm from a dairy, remember? Go on."

When I returned with the pan of mash he was working with her carefully. He glanced up at me. "Get up by her head and talk to her. Calm her. I have to reach in and see if the calf's twisted."

"Twisted. Oh, Toby—"

"Go on. If it's got a leg turned, I might be able to help."

So I held the cow's head in my lap and talked to her, stroking her face and ears. I said a lot of nonsense to her about how lovely her calf would be, a heifer of course, and how beautiful she was. Finally she quieted.

Toby worked for some time. From time to time I heard him grunt, and I realized that though he was mostly healed, twisting oneself around a laboring cow still placed a lot of strain on a body.

He muttered something I couldn't catch, then sat back on his heels and shoved heavy dark hair out of his face with a forearm.

"She should be all right now."

"Did you fix it?"

"The calf had a leg turned, like I thought. I pulled it straight, so I think you'll have yourself a new mouth to feed pretty quick."

"Not me," I said happily. "Princess will have the feeding to do."

The cow settled into rhythmic breathing, contracted her flanks a couple of times, then gave a tremendous push. She lifted her head and peered at her hindquarters.

I moved and knelt next to Toby in the straw, looking down in wonder on the little calf. It was wet and slimy, still encased in its sac, but Princess broke it with her tongue. She got up with a heaving effort and began to lick the creature dry with her tongue.

Toby was tired. "It's a heifer. What you wanted."

"Toby," I said gently, "Oh Toby." I beamed at him. "Thank you!"

I threw my arms around him and hugged him with all the gratitude in my body. Trouble was, he didn't realize it was gratitude.

I disentangled myself rapidly as he pulled me close. I avoided his kiss but was completely aware of the pressure of his arms around me. I pulled away and sat staring at him.

"I was only thanking you," I said unsteadily.

He grinned companionably back. "Like I thanked you."

I felt the heat in my face. "But—I didn't mean—"

"Lonnie, it doesn't matter. Whatever your reasons, the result suits me fine."

"Toby, you don't understand. . . ."

He got to his feet. "Yes, I do." He reached down and pulled me up, smiling warmly at me. "You don't yet, maybe, but you will. I'm willing to wait."

I stared searchingly at him, exploring my feelings, but got no answer. He reached out and tugged gently at my braid, like my pa used to do, but there was nothing fatherly about it.

Oh my sweet Lord, I thought to myself, what have I gotten myself into?

I stepped away abruptly, shutting off all the

bewildering emotions flooding through me. My hands were fists and my whole body felt stiff.

"Toby, there's an end to it."

He stared solemnly back at me, then nodded. "Maybe there is. For now."

"For good," I snapped, then glanced back at the little calf. I sighed and relaxed. "Thanks for helping the cow."

In the morning he came out to the garden and stared down at me as I weeded. Finally I sat back and tucked my legs beneath me.

"Something troubling you, Toby?"

"You always know, don't you?"

"You're wearing a very long face."

"Why didn't you ask where I went? All last night over supper, afterward when we talked over what the heifer meant to you. Why didn't you ask?"

I found a stick and picked at the dirt, avoiding his beseeching eyes. "It's your concern. You say you treasure your freedom, and freedom is being able to leave when you want." I slid a glance at him. "Ain't that what you say?"

"Isn't." He dropped to the ground and met my gaze on a common level. "I've said it. I meant it."

"Meant?"

He also found a twig and began excavating. We were both horribly uncomfortable, searching for an easier way. The world was closing in on me.

"I couldn't help but recall what Dan Michael said. About you telling me to go soon," he said quietly. "So I decided to do it when you weren't around. I thought it would be easier that way."

"Why should it be?"

"Don't you understand?" he whispered. "I was walking out on *you*."

"You can't walk out on something you never had," I said firmly. "Go your own way, Toby. It's what you've always wanted."

"But I don't anymore."

"You're a fool."

It startled him. "Why a fool?"

"Only a fool gives up on a dream so quick." I smiled at him, feeling strangely content. "I've done the thinking you told me I should. I started dreaming again, just a little. Such things can be good, when you've got the time."

He was beginning to smile himself. "Then you don't think little of me for leaving?"

My stomach fluttered into an odd calmness, a confidence I was beginning to understand. What's more, I was beginning to like it.

"Toby—" I paused—"You came back, didn't you?"

It surprised us both. He sat there, silent, and I suddenly became quite busy weeding. I thought I was doing just fine until I realized I was busily pulling bean sprouts instead of weeds. Hastily I tried to stick them back in the ground, but it was too late. Finally I dropped everything and stared helplessly at the ground, forlorn and lost within a soul I no longer understood.

"Then it's settled," he said calmly.

"What is?" I demanded hurriedly, unsure of his proprietary tone.

He rose, towering over me. I shielded my eyes against the sun as I peered up at him.

"I'll be staying on."

"You'll be *what?*"

"Staying."

I got to my feet, glaring at him, hands on hips. "What *for*, in the name of God?"

He smiled sadly at me. "Until you admit it for what it is, let's just say I'll stay on to pay off the debt I owe you."

"You don't owe me a thing," I said quickly. "It wasn't any trouble."

"Lonnie, don't be a fool."

I gaped at him as he started to turn away. "A fool! You're calling me a fool? Toby Markham . . ." I hurried to catch up to him as he moved to the house.

He turned on me at the doorway. "Lonnie, I'm staying!"

I watched him stomp into the house, furious with himself and me, and then I turned away and wandered back to the garden. I sat down in the dirt and contemplated my spirits, still stunned by his forceful entrance back into my life.

What bothered me most was the overwhelming relief I felt. Toby had chosen to stay.

The evenings turned cool and each night after supper we sat in the front room and traded our thoughts on things we believed in. We got along comfortably, and I began to see what it meant to have a man to share things with. The work was easier, though I refused to let him do it all.

The debt, I thought, would surely be paid by winter. And then he would go. California, perhaps, maybe Colorado. Gold and silver lured them all, and I wondered how much longer he would willingly shoulder my burden.

The day Toby swore to stand by me if the bank came after my land made me realize how closely he'd bound himself to my future. It frightened me. I was not willing to let him into the major part of my life. I was incapable to much feeling past my love for the land. He didn't touch me again and never forced intimacy on me, but there was an unspoken acceptance on his part that it was only a matter of time. Stubbornly I refused to consider it, even within my heart. Toby had come for a while, and then he would go.

He made me recall the happier times of my life: the evenings my family had spent after supper, talking of things to come. I had pushed those memories away so the pain would diminish, but suddenly I wanted all of them back. Toby fit in, and I accepted him.

The thunderstorm rolled in as I wandered along the river bank, picking healing herbs I wanted to dry and store away. The air became turbulent and dark, and heat built on my skin. The morning turned sour, humid, closing in to oppress the earth. The clouds massed overhead, deep pockets of maddened blackness roiling in scalloped gray. The locusts stilled against the mounting threat of rain.

I thought the storm might ease the hot and heavy stillness like a punctured boil. When it came, it came

139

with fury.

I stood in the deluge, uncaring of the wet. At first it was a hot storm, then cooled and chased away the brooding heaviness. I peered upward to watch the rain fall, then tucked my head down as it began to fall like a soaked sheet.

Lightning split the sky apart like a black wound cleansed by cautery. Suddenly frightened, I cried out and ran for the house, tossing away the herbs I'd picked.

The soaked grass dragged at my legs as I ran, slapping at me as if it would pull me down. The thick growth hid the log, and when I sprawled over it I fell with the heaviness of death.

And it all came back.

The smell hit me first, the stench of burning meat. One of the cows had not gotten away when the scavengers fired the lean-to, and the smell of charring beef was hidden by the acrid stench of shriveling hide. The mule streaked by me in terror, followed by my pa's brown saddle mare. Wood smoke boiled into the air, and with it went the scent of burning animals. I shrieked something and ran on.

My pa lay by the well, rifle clutched in his hands. His face was turned away from me, but the blood clotted on the back of his head. I stumbled away, gagging, and found my mother in the doorway.

She wasn't screaming anymore. She was silenced. I saw the bloodstains across her dress and knew I'd never hear her again.

My sister lay beside her, and my baby brother whimpered when I knelt by him on the rug. I lifted his broken body in my arms, and then he died.

*And I stared up at the roof and cried out my pain
and fear.*

Toby dragged me up from the earth and held me in
his arms. I shuddered against him silently, fighting
back the painful sobs. I became aware that he spoke
soothingly to me, pushing away my fears, helping
me back to myself.

I subsided and let him hold me, grateful for his
care. The storm beat down upon us both, and it was a
cleansing rain. When I finally drew back from his
chest I felt released.

"Have you never cried for them before?" he asked
gently.

I stared at him, subdued by my outburst. "How did
you know?"

He pushed wet hair away from my face. "You were
screaming about your brother, Lonnie. How you
asked God to save him and still he died."

"I'm sorry," I whispered in horror.

"Don't be. You needed this. It's been a long time
coming."

I looked into his face and saw what I'd been afraid
to see before. He was more than carefree, careless
soul. He was compassion and strength and I needed
him.

But still I pulled away.

"Lonnie, there's something I must say."

"No."

He laughed. "How do you know what I intend to
tell you?"

"I don't, but I don't want to hear it anyway. Just

in case."

"In case of what?"

"In case you say something foolish."

"I've done it before."

"Let's not get into a habit of it."

"All I want to say—"

"No!" I said violently. "Let me go."

He did not release my arms. "Give it up this once, Lonnie."

I swallowed, avoiding his eyes. "Give what up?"

"That high, prickly pride of yours. Just this once let it go, and admit you care."

"For you?" I snapped, and regretted it instantly.

"For yourself, Lonnie. You. You can't care for me until you care for yourself."

"Myself?" I whispered, stricken by his words.

"You've locked yourself away. For two years you've hounded yourself into living apart. You've made yourself believe you needed no one."

"You," I said clearly, "are a drifter and a wanderer with no desire for roots. You've spent some time here, healing, and now you try to tell me you care, and that I should care for you. Leave it alone, Toby. You'll be gone with the next rain."

"No."

Suddenly I was desperate. *"Why?* Why do you want to do this?"

"For God's sake, girl, I want to marry you!"

I was cold. I got to my feet and stood over him, hugging myself against the chill. I felt myself tremble and tried to dismiss it, but it went bone-deep.

"Toby, you can't."

"Can't what? Can't marry you, or can't want to?"

"Both," I said numbly.

He laughed and slicked away the rain from his eyes. "Of course I can. Lonnie, are you a girl who wants to be told a man loves her before she consents to a wedding?"

"A wedding?"

"It's generally a good idea."

"*Why?*"

He shrugged as I latched onto the tree, seeking strength. "I want to set my roots. Nail my boots to the floor." He grinned brilliantly. "I want to do exactly what I said I wouldn't do."

I glared at him. "I don't believe you. It ain't possible."

"Why not?"

"You hardly know me." I glared at him. "Nor do I know you."

He rose, folding his arms. "I know enough of you, Lonnie Ryan. I know enough to know."

"You're a fool," I said desperately. "A lightminded fool who doesn't know *what* he wants."

"I've said I'll marry you!" he cried angrily. "What else do you want?"

Fear beat hollowly in my heart. "I don't know. Please—I don't know."

"Oh, Lonnie, did you think you'd never love anyone?"

The tree bark bit into my palms as I pressed my hands against it. "I *have* loved! For God's sake, let me be! I have loved, and they died! I lost it all once, how could I risk it again?" I stared at him through tears

143

that fell with the rain on my face. "How can I risk losing you?"

He pulled me from the tree and took me in his arms. He spoke very softly against my head. "Let it be, Lonnie, let it be. I won't force you."

"Just let me go, Toby."

He did, and I went slowly to the house.

Chapter Nine

The clouds broke up and the storm moved on, but the heaviness it left settled into my bones and mind. I brooded silently, feeling a quiet dread. Toby had destroyed my equilibrium.

I realized two years alone on the High Plains had taught me to deal with quite a lot. With nearly everything. Everything but a man.

He took it well. Perhaps he realized what kind of thoughts and fears he'd put into my head. I began to see he really did know me. Instinctively he knew when to speak and when to keep silent. Somehow we muddled through the day.

Supper was quiet. Nothing was said of his declaration. Yet when I did slip and meet his eyes I saw many words reflected there, words he wanted to speak, but saying nothing because I refused to hear. The air was drawn and tense between us, charged with unspoken feelings. The food was tasteless in my mouth.

After supper Toby went to the rocker and sat, dark-browed as he stared off into space. His face was kept expressionless, but I watched furtively, expecting a change.

At last he broke the silence, his words a welcome release. He spoke calmly and without emotion.

"If you have paper and a pen, I'd like to write my mother. She would want to know about my plans."

I turned from the sink. "There is no paper. But I'll go to town tomorrow and fetch some."

He shrugged. "Don't go to the trouble. I can do without."

"I don't mind the drive. I'll go."

His warm smile flashed and brought relief to me. "Good. I'll go with you."

"You can't!" I said quickly.

The bright cast of his face altered. "You don't want me anywhere near you, do you?"

"Oh, it ain't that. No, Toby. It's for safety's sake I want you here."

"Safety's sake?"

"If folks in town see you with me, you can be certain they'll point a finger to the farm when the Barstows come."

Incredulously I watched dawning realization in his eyes. He had forgotten all about the men chasing him. In the face of what he had said to me about marriage, he'd utterly neglected his circumstances.

"Yes," he said soberly, "you're right. I—I hadn't realized." He swallowed. "Are they so close to Ridgely?"

I met his solemn eyes across the room. "They're due any day, Toby."

"Then I'd best stay here."

"Yes."

He stirred in the rocker, stroking Patch as the cat

leaped into his lap. "You'd best stay, too. I don't want you getting into trouble."

"I can't hide here," I said gently. "They'll come sooner or later. I'd rather face them in town where there's people I know, instead of meeting them here."

He smiled across at me lopsidedly. "You said once the Barstows didn't scare you. Did you mean it?"

I hunched a shoulder. "I don't know. I'd be a fool to say flat out I'm not frightened of what they are, but maybe it'll help me stand up to them. Sometimes fear makes a good strengthener. Any timid thing will fight if backed into a corner."

"I'd hardly call you timid."

I grinned at him, pleased the easiness was back. "Stubborn might be a better word for me."

"Stubbornness makes for strength, too."

"I suppose." I sighed and rubbed distractedly at my forehead. "Toby, I'm going to bed. Sleep well."

He frowned. "It's early yet."

"I'm tired. Wearied to the bone. And I've got a lot of thinking to do."

"About what?"

I halted at the curtained doorway of my tiny bedroom and glanced at him over a shoulder. "You laid a heaviness on my soul today in the rain. Now let me think it over."

Color came up in his strong-boned face and light swelled in his eyes. "You mean you'll really consider it?"

"I'm not *considering* anything," I explained. "I'm only trying to get my thoughts straight. You muddled everything up today."

"Getting married isn't like a sickness, Lonnie, you

147

don't die from it."

I glared at him, then tried to sound patient. "These things don't come easy to me. You know that."

"I know it well."

I took a deep breath, trembling, making an effort to ignore my weariness. I was still very hesitant about the new meaning creeping into my life, but I had to tell him something. I had to let him know.

"It wouldn't be fair, you know, not fair at all—if I said I couldn't *ever* love you."

Silence fell between us. I could feel my heavy heartbeat and wondered if Toby could hear it clear across the room. His head lifted and his eyes met mine. For a long moment all we could do was stare at one another. Then he began to smile.

"Perhaps I must be patient."

I moved across the room and stood before him. "I know it's less than you wanted, but it's more than I ever expected to give. Would you put words in my mouth?"

"Never."

"Then let me be to think."

He grinned. "And the considering part will come later?"

I laughed at him, then shivered once. "Sleep well, Toby."

I took myself off to bed but sleep wouldn't come. My thoughts were disjointed, skipping around so much I could not pin anything down. I tossed the covers off, hot in the rain-washed night, unable to find a comfortable position. My eyes burned with grit and my head felt tight, pressing in against my brain. I heard Toby go to bed at last, and when dawn came in

I found I hadn't slept at all. I could feel every lost minute.

I lay staring at the roof, disinclined to get out of bed. It was past time for me to start the chores, but for once I couldn't dredge up the vitality to climb out of bed and start work.

Toby finally came to the doorway and pulled the curtain aside. "Are you awake?"

I swallowed, startled at the soreness it caused. "I'm awake," I rasped.

"Are you getting up?"

"I am up." I crawled out of bed.

Once dressed I went in to the table, aware of the ache in my bones. Even my skin hurt. I sat down quickly as my head went oddly light and woolly. I muttered to myself, not even understanding my own words. Toby came out of the bedroom.

"Are you all right?"

"I'm fine. Fine. Just tired."

He came around the table and stared at me. "You look sick."

"I'm never sick," I said, shivering once.

"You better go back to bed."

"Chores," I croaked. I felt drained, sucked dry of all strength. All I wanted to do was lie down on the floor and let the world go away.

"I can do the chores, Lonnie. Go back to bed."

I leaned my head on my arms, peering up through squinted eyes at his concerned face. "I've got things to do. I have to go into town and get your paper."

"Forget that." He sat down next to me and looked closely at my face, which felt hot. "You'll do better off in bed."

"I don't take orders from you."

He ignored that. "You look terrible."

I was feeling worse by the moment and hearing that helped me none at all. I flashed him a resentful look and pushed to my feet, steadying myself against the table. Toby caught my arm and ignored me as I tried to pull away.

"Let's get you to bed."

I quit arguing and let him forcibly take me off to bed. I crawled in and huddled beneath the covers, hoping my stomach would stop its heaving.

"Toby," I said weakly, "Go away and leave me alone."

"I want to help."

"Then bring me my chamber pot and go away. Far."

"Oh," he said sharply, and did as I asked.

When I awoke I was a huddled mass of misery beneath my blankets. I wanted to die. I, who was never sick, felt so bad I understood what it was to need attention and care. But I wouldn't ask for it from him. It went against my nature.

"Toby!" My own cry woke me, startling me, but not nearly as much as the conviction he was gone. He had left again, this time for good, and I struggled up on one elbow. I would get up and go after him, fetching him back for good. I did not want him to leave me.

He came and leaned over me. "Lonnie," he whispered, "rest easy. I'm right here."

"You left me," I told him fearfully. "Like before. You left." I stared up into his face, searching it for the truth. "You were gone."

150

"No, no, I've been here all the time. It's only a dream."

My hand reached out for his arm, and he grasped it gently, moving to sit down next to me.

"Toby, you won't go?"

"I won't go."

"Toby, don't ever go."

Gently he smoothed back my damp hair. "I won't. I promise."

I was fading, drifting away. My voice was hardly a sound. "I don't want you to go."

"You're stuck with me, Lonnie. Like it or not."

My hand fell away from his and I slept.

He was not in the house when I awoke. The fever had gone and I felt well, if worn out, but I was suddenly afraid.

I got out of bed and changed, moving slowly but enough to get it done. Finally I walked carefully across the floor and out the front door. Fear still washed at me in waves, a twofold fear. One was that Toby had gone, another that it upset me so. How had I let myself get trapped?

I found him at the lean-to, milking Princess. He spoke softly to the cow, praising her fine little calf and predicting great things for the two of them. I stood silently in the doorway, struck by the tableau and not wishing to ruin it. I couldn't help but notice the content look on his face, and the gentleness with which he worked.

Patch was there demanding his share, and Toby obliged with a quick squirt from the teat. His aim was better than mine. Then he rose and lifted the brimming bucket. He halted when he saw me, his face flooding with surprise and embarrassment. I grinned at him.

"You enjoyed that, Toby. You with all your talk of hating dairy work."

He smiled sheepishly. "I never hated milking. Just the other work."

"I see."

"Besides, someone had to do it while you were sick." He peered at me. "Are you better? You look a little peaked."

"I'm wobbly, but well. Come on, let's go get some breakfast. I'm starved."

He grinned teasingly. "That's because you spent most of the last two days losing everything you ever ate."

I flushed and turned away, stiffening my back. I heard his laughter as I marched toward the house, and he came along behind.

Breakfast was a silent affair. I avoided his eyes and did some deep thinking, for I'd been able to straighten a few things in my head as I lay under the covers. I knew Toby well enough to realize he wanted me for me, not the land. Billy Ringling, a farmboy who lived west of me, had offered for me once. I'd learned real quick that as a wife I was worth forty acres of prime land and a good house. I told Billy Ringling off and hadn't thought of marriage since, except to know it wasn't for me. I'd never thought it could be.

And now Toby Markham came busting into my life with his bright dreams and quick words and the subject came up all over again. It was easy for me to deny it obstinately, particularly to myself. I'd done well enough without a man, why should I need one now?

But my soul whispered to me that this was Toby, and Toby was entirely different. Well, so was I. It aggravated me that I even had to think about the thing. Always before, decisions came fast to me, particularly the ones I said no to, but this was different.

I'd grown used to his presence. I liked working with him, being with him, seeing what our combined efforts produced. I liked cooking for us both and watching him fill up on my food, and I especially liked sitting after supper listening to him talk about his hopes for the future, when they didn't include me. Whenever *I* came into it I was wary as a wolf cub with a bone.

He was forever telling me how to improve the place, how to make changes and improvements, extend the fields, increase the profits, add new crops. For a man who hated farming, he knew what the life was.

But I was afraid. I'd lost one beloved family; I couldn't do it again. I'd have nothing left save the land, and as much as it meant to me, I didn't think I had strength enough to face such a loss again. I had been alone and lonely too long. I wanted Toby's company, but I was afraid to lose him still. It wasn't marriage I was afraid of, it was the end of it.

He ate well. His color was good and he'd filled out, replacing the weight he'd lost. He was healed. It was time for him to go. I had said all along he must leave when he was healthy, and now I couldn't let him. I sighed and pushed my plate away.

"Toby, I've done my considering."

His chewing slowed as he looked at me. After a moment he swallowed, then sipped at coffee to wash his meal down. I saw a new wariness in his eyes I'd never seen before, and I realized my actions meant as much to him as they did me. Slowly he set the mug down and folded his arms on the table.

"So. I'm to know if I have a home or must move on again."

"You've got a home in Minnesota," I snapped.

He smiled faintly. "I left it behind. Right now I have none."

"Whose fault is that?"

"Lonnie—"

"All right," I sighed, giving it up. "All right, I'll quit belaboring the point. But it ain't easy."

"Isn't."

"Ain't!" I exclaimed. "If you're so all-fired sure you want me for a wife, you'd best get used to my ways of speech and habits. You remind me of my ma, always on me about proper speech."

He smiled. "Lonnie, I think you're not ready to say what you want to say. I understand. It's like you said, I laid a heaviness on your soul."

I swallowed, unaccountably relieved. "I thought I might go into town today."

"Are you well enough?"

"I feel fine, and I'd like to go. Maybe I can sort things out on the way in. I'll give you an answer when I get back."

154

His expression was odd. "Lonnie, I've never known anyone like you. Most people you can predict what they might say or do, but you—well, let's just say I'd expect anything out of you. You might say yes to me, but you might just as easily say no." He shook his head. "I just don't know."

"Remember that," I said quietly.

He rose. "I'll go hitch up the buckboard."

I gathered up the money I needed and rebraided my hair, for once deciding I should take a little care with my appearance. It wasn't every day I considered a proposal. I grinned lopsidedly at myself in the vanity glass. My Lord, what would I do with a proposal every day?

Tracker waited impatiently at the buckboard as I walked out to it. I set the rifle beneath the seat as always and sent the hound to his regular place. I nearly tripped over Patch, who wound himself around my bare legs and Toby's booted feet.

Toby helped me into the buckboard. I nearly stumbled in the doing of it, for I was used to managing on my own. I shot him a startled glance and saw his amused smile, but he said nothing of it and neither did I. I wasn't much of a lady, I guess, but there was no help for it. I gathered up the reins and looked at him.

"I'm going."

"If you come to any decisions out there on the prairie, hurry back."

I shook my head at him. "You're too impatient. For all you know I might send you from my land."

"Maybe," he said quietly, "but I don't think so."

155

I felt my face redden. "You're too certain of yourself!"

"A man has to be, with you."

I ignored the glint in his eyes and slapped the reins down on the mare's back to send her off. My back was rigid as I left the yard, certain Toby had overstepped his bounds. He had no right—well, maybe. I glanced back and saw him staring after me. With a sudden wash of happiness I considered the feeling of having someone waiting for me. It made me feel special. I liked that.

My bare feet were planted against the rough wood of the tilted front board and my toes curled against the splintery surface as I did the sorting out I needed. The leather reins lay loose in my hands, bobbing and slacking with the mare's motion, shifting against my callused palms. I loved the language of the road.

Listening to Toby's hopes in life, and the dreams, had made me alter some of my own convictions. I was no longer the same girl. I always thought I'd hate losing a part of myself, but this was different. Life alone loomed bleak, empty, unfulfilled. I no longer cherished the solitude I had cloaked myself in to stave off the piercing loneliness. Solitude had been a way of survival then, and I had welcomed it, but it was welcome no longer.

I knew there would be a great deal of learning involved. And a greater need for patience and tolerance. We were both prideful and prickly to a fault, always quick to hackle. But it was plumb foolish to deny the only man I could wish to share my life with was Toby. So I quit denying it, and accepted it.

The turmoil slid away. Intense relief flooded through me, leaving me weakly surprised at my response. I hadn't been fighting Toby, I'd been fighting myself.

"Lonnie Ryan, you've been a fool," I said to myself, and was content.

Chapter Ten

The mare's pricking ears brought me back to earth.
I found we had reached the edge of Ridgely while I
stayed deep in my thoughts. My decision reached, I
looked at the town through new eyes and found
everything brighter and more interesting. It was the
same town, but I wasn't the same person. Everything
seemed better.

Tracker barked and nearly startled me off the seat. I
hushed him, once my heart settled down, and saw a
mottled brown dog streak across the dusty street to
reach shade beneath the boardwalk in front of Mick's
saloon.

I halted the mare before Larsson's store and
climbed down, tying her off. Tracker suddenly
growled menacingly and nearly lunged out of the
buckboard. I whirled and took a step backward as the
old man lurched up against the hitch rail, clutching
at it. He wavered on his feet and I knew if he let go
he'd fall in a dusty heap, but he had a death grip on
the rail.

I put a hand out to Tracker and hushed him
quietly. The old man was harmless. The whole town

knew that.

Ridgely called him Rainmaker. His real name had been lost for years, and I don't think anyone recalled it. Long ago he'd learned to answer to the new title. Now he was part of the woodwork. The town drunk, and a pitiful example of a life gone wrong. He was the butt of jokes, a target for small boys with slingshots, and an example of a man fouled by the hazards of drink which the farmwomen loved to use to their husbands. Rainmaker would do nearly anything for the price of a drink. Occasionally he managed to scrape together a few coins, Mick would take pity on him, and Rainmaker would have his bottle of whisky.

He was an old man grown ancient, withered by drink and poor diet. His blue eyes were red-rimmed, rheumy, his skin parchment yellow. He licked his lips constantly and wiped his nose on the sleeve of his frayed black suit coat.

Once it had been a proud suit for a proud man, but over the years it had become stained and torn, faded with exposure to dust, sun and filth. Straggly gray hair hung to his shoulders and his beard was matted and foul. He wore an old stovepipe hat crushed many times with many falls, but it sat atop his head in the remains of his tattered pride. Once he had been important; once he had been valued. Once he had even been highly paid for his services.

I knew the story well. It was told to every stranger who unwittingly asked his name. Years before Ridgely and most of Macklin County had lain dying of thirst, drowning in dusty drought. Fierce sun baked the land and burned the crops, drying the waterholes and killing the stock. People pulled out with what they could salvage, heading back East or further west in hopes of finding water. The river by my farm had fouled itself with minerals, undrinkable. For nearly four months rain was denied to the Kansas High Plains.

Rainmaker came riding into Ridgely on a tall red peddler's wagon with a team of shiny black horses pulling it proudly. He was known as *the* Rainmaker then, and he claimed he could cause the rain to fall. Everyone was so desperate for water they agreed to pay his price.

Children, men and women begged him to make the rains come and take away the drought. For three days he called out mystical, magical words to the sky, casting powders into a fire and sending stinking smoke upwards. Folks ran back and forth, seeing he had both food and drink, doing whatever he asked. A smart man might have said Rainmaker was only taking advantage of the situation, but there were no smart men left. Everyone was too desperate.

Four days later the rains came. Rainmaker, I had heard, was just as surprised as everyone else. He was no magic man, but the storm sweeping in across the prairie saved his head. He was proclaimed a savior, and in the generous gratitude of the townsfolk, Rainmaker reveled.

Whisky was made free to him, and by the time the adulation wore away and his popularity became a thing of the past, he loved it too much. He stayed on, begging for drinks. His fine horses were sold, his bright wagon dismantled, and Rainmaker became the town drunk.

I watched the old man put out a gnarled hand, trembling and heavily veined. I could smell him from two feet away, and it made me want to retch.

"Whisky," he wheezed at me through yellowed and broken teeth. "Whisky."

"Do your asking someplace else," I told him. "You won't get anything from me. I ain't got a penny to spare, Rainmaker."

His eyes were pleading. "I'll brush your horse—I'll water him. Let me do something—something—earn a drink of whisky."

"Not from me." I shook my head. "I've got nothing for you to do."

"Please, please . . ." He hung onto the hitch rail, nearly grovelling in the dust.

I backed a step away. "I can't help you. Maybe someone else can."

I couldn't comfortably feel pity for the old man. Pity was a thing I'd fought against for myself too long. I found it a cloying and sickening emotion, whatever the cause for it. I'd give none to him.

"Whisky—I need whisky. I'll water your horse—feed your horse . . ."

I sighed and shook my head as the trembling hand reached out. "No. I'm sorry."

Tracker watched every move made by the old man, wary of him. Suddenly Rainmaker's attention found the hound and I saw a brightness come into his watery eyes for the first time.

"A dog. I had a dog once." He smiled in childish wonder. "Once, I had a dog. He was a real nice dog. This one looks like he's a nice dog. Is he?"

I felt sickened and saddened. He was so lonely.

161

"He's a good dog, Rainmaker."

"I had a dog once." Abruptly the light faded from his eyes. "But he died. I had him since he was a pup. A long time. But he died." He heaved an immense sigh. "He was a nice dog."

The old man was crying. Hacking sobs came out of his chest and rolled down his withered cheeks. I felt a horrible welling of emotion in my chest and backed up yet another step. I mustn't let the old man get through my shell of confidence.

"I can't give you anything, Rainmaker. I've got nothing. Go ask someone else."

I ducked under the rail and stepped up on the boardwalk, looking back to see what the old man would do. He still clutched at the hitch rail with one hand, but reached out to Tracker with the other. His voice was choked and broken as he spoke to the hound, repeating himself childishly.

"I had a dog once, a nice dog. You're a nice dog, too."

Suppressing a shiver down my spine, I turned and went into the store.

Larsson looked up instantly as I swung open the door and the naked expression of fear on his face stopped me cold. Abruptly he smiled, set down his books, and came around the counter.

"Lonnie! It's good to see you again so soon!"

I stepped in and let the door swing shut behind me, ringing the silver bell. The Swede's greeting was done in great relief, and I wondered what had caused it.

"I've come in for writing paper," I explained. "Come to think of it, I need ink too."

He smiled and adjusted his spectacles. "Are you writing to someone in Ohio?"

I felt suddenly cold. I hadn't thought what my request might do. "No." I tried a weak smile. "There's no one in Ohio for me. It's—it's an advertisement I saw in an old catalogue of my ma's. A dress. I thought—I thought I might send for the pattern."

It was a very poor explanation, but the best I could do. Larsson nodded at me, seeming to accept it, but I wondered what was on his mind. Normally he chatted with me if he was alone, and now he merely treated me like a customer.

"I'll find you the paper and ink."

He began sorting through things by his counter, and I wandered around to look at things. Part of me wanted to tell him about Toby and my big decision, but I didn't dare. Larsson was skittish enough about something; he didn't need me bothering him. Besides, the fewer people knew about Toby the better. Even my friends.

I was far back in the store looking at some good leather belts with silver buckles when the door opened hurriedly, banging the bell. I looked up and saw Abner Barton shutting the door as if to lock out the world. Larsson instantly stopped digging through his papers, freezing in place.

"Olaf, have they come in here yet?" Barton demanded.

Larsson shook his head. "Not here, not yet. You think men such as they might come in a *store*?"

Barton sighed heavily, worriedly, and pushed grimy fingers through what hair he had left. He

163

shook his head slowly, like a confused bull.

"I don't know, Olaf. How can I say? I think men like them would go anywhere and do anything, if it suited their purpose. Even it it meant tearing the town apart."

"Then they must still be in the saloon."

"Two of them walked out of Mick's a minute ago. I reckon they're commencing to go building by building, now they've whet their thirst." He sent a searching look around the store, but it was quick and missed me. "I'll go next door and check on things."

The Swede nodded. "Good, make certain all are fine. I'll tell someone if I have any trouble here."

I stepped forward before the blacksmith could leave. "Mr. Barton. Wait."

He swung back around, startled to see me as I came forward into the light. "Lonnie!" Shock and concern mingled on his broad face. "Lonnie—"

"It's them, ain't it?" I asked evenly. "The Barstows."

Barton glanced sharply at the silent Swede. Slowly he looked back at me and smoothed his big hands down the front of his leather apron. His voice was calm, but it took effort on his part to keep it that way.

"Now, Lonnie, there's nothing for you to fret about."

"I'm not fretting. I'm asking."

He was uncomfortable. "This is serious."

"I'm being serious. Either you tell me, or I'll go ask someone else."

"All right," he said on a heavy breath. "Yes, it's the Barstow gang. Come to find the man who got Ben Barstow hanged."

164

I shrugged lightly. "We expected them to show up. You said so yourself."

His face was hard, his voice harder still. "Nothing seems real until trouble arrives in the flesh. Now they're here; everyone's walking scared. I'll make my offer again, Lonnie. Come out to the house and stay with Emily and the boys."

"Thank you, but no."

His eyes pleaded with me. "Please, Lonnie."

"They'll do me no harm. Why should they?"

He looked helplessly at Larsson, who shook his head and shrugged. There was nothing either of them could say.

"All right," Barton said at last. "Just be careful. And if you need help—"

"I know," I said quietly. "I'll come to you."

Larsson started in on me the moment Barton left the store. His pale eyes were serious behind his spectacles. "You should have gone with him. Abner is a good man. He'd make certain nothing would happen to you."

"I'll look after myself. I always do." I smiled to take the sting out of my rude words. "Can I have my paper and ink, please?"

A great sadness settled in his eyes and he nodded, searching through his things again. Finally he came up with some clean sheets of paper and a bottle of black ink. I went over to inspect my purchase and dug out my coins.

He smiled at me. "You want sealing wax and a stamp so it goes where you want? To that catalogue place?"

"Oh, I guess so. You better add those in." I counted

out my coins. "Do I have enough?"

"You have enough. More than you need. Here, I'll wrap it up for you."

I pushed the coins across the counter as he wrapped everything up in a packet of brown parcel paper. I took it and opened my mouth to thank him, but he was paying no mind at all.

I realized the bell on the door had rung, and I turned to see who it was.

Two of the Barstows stood there, slouching against the door.

I knew instantly they were a part of the gang. They weren't farmers, weren't cowboys. What they were was becoming abundantly clear, and I felt a quick fear spring up in my belly.

One was dressed as if for church. More likely a funeral, I thought, wondering whose it might be. Except for the blue of his shirt and the oddly bright, clear blue of his eyes, he wore black. He even wore a vest shining with silver buttons.

A fine layer of dust lay over his clothing, but it didn't detract from his uncommon good looks. He was almost pretty, like a girl, but there was a man behind it all. His were the sort of looks that would send a saloon girl swooning, and even a proper lady might spare him a glance. But I knew he was a killer. It showed in every inch of him, an arrogant assurance of ability.

I felt a chill slide down my spine as I looked at his handsome face and curly black hair. A curling of revulsion came into my belly. He was young, self-content, vividly alive, and there was something very wrong about him.

The other was younger, maybe Toby's age. There was nothing quiet or spooky about him. His blue eyes were bold and his grin cocky. He wasn't bad-favored either, but his face was wide open with youthful brashness, not the refined clarity of his companion's.

He wore a tan hat with a long, yellow feather tucked in the band around the crown, and as he looked around the store I realized who he was. Jordy Macklin.

I wanted badly to get out of the store and go home, but they blocked the door and I wasn't about to go closer. I tried to appear unruffled and unimpressed, like such men walked into the store every day, but my heart banged against my ribs and my belly turned over.

Then Larsson broke the stillness. "Can I help you with anything?" His voice was high and quavery, but I doubted *I* could even get a word out.

The one I called Jordy took a few steps forward, moving loose-jointed, glancing around at everything with bright interest. He fussed with the long tie-strings of his hat as they dangled against his shirt.

He said nothing. I watched him move around the store, inspecting things, picking them up and setting them back down. Finally he shook his head and grinned at the Swede, displaying deep dimples.

"Well now, old man, you figure you got what we want?"

Larsson licked his lips. "What is it you need?"

Jordy looked the Swede straight in the eye. "It ain't what we need, old man, it's what we want. Whatever strikes our fancy."

Larsson tried to remain calm and was hard-pressed to do it. I saw the conflict in his face; he wanted to order them from his store but realized the folly in it. Why antagonize men like them?

"Then tell me what I can help you with. Maybe I got it here."

Jordy ignored him and continued to wander his way through the store. He brushed by me closely, purposely, slanting me a glinting sideways look, but I stood my ground. I was determined not to flinch under his amused glance.

As Jordy passed I looked over at his gunfighter-friend and saw the pearl-handled gun at his hip. I wondered how many people he'd killed.

He stood silently, relaxed, but his bright eyes were intent on everything Jordy did. I felt him look at me, right through me, and nearly shivered beneath his stare. He had the kind of eyes that could rob a man of his soul. "Lacklander," I whispered in my mind. Wes Lacklander. Had to be. Barstow and Gibbs were older, Loggins had told me so. Wes Lacklander, who was crazy in the head and liked to kill women when he used them.

A deadly cold stole into my bones. He studied me the way a man might a horse. A sickened, dry-mouthed fear shot through my body.

Jordy paused in his wanderings and reached into the big barrel of crackers Larsson left out for folks. He left flaky crumbs all over as he moved on. His spurs chinked against the floor, rolling as he moved. There was a rhythm in his walk, though his steps were lazy. The spurs rolled across the wood floor, ringing and chinking as he stepped out again. The noise was loud in my ears.

When he reached the candy counter he helped himself to a generous handful of long, black licorice whips.

"Hey, Wes." Jordy abruptly shifted his attention to his silent friend. "You see anything in here you want?"

Lacklander appeared bored by the matter, but his eyes were alive in his fair face. He stared at me and smiled a little, his voice husky and deep.

"Just one thing."

Jordy hooted, breaking the heavy stillness of the store. He walked over to me and slid in behind, running a thumb down my back. I stiffened and shrugged away from it, but he only laughed.

"She's a mite scrawny, Wes. Not a whole lot of meat on her bones. You like 'em with a little more flesh to 'em."

I thanked God for my angular shape and lean bones.

Lacklander shrugged eloquently. "No matter."

Larsson sounded frightened. He knew something had gone violently wrong. "Leave her alone!"

Jordy grinned. "Old man, you can't tell us what to do." He clicked his tongue in shame. "Don't you know who we are?"

The Swede nodded jerkily and his spectacles slid down his nose. He shoved them back up. "I know who you be. You be part of Matt Barstow's boys. Everyone in town knows you've come. For no good!"

Jordy's eyes narrowed. "Old man, to you it's *Mister* Barstow. Understand? Let's have a little more manners, here."

"I hear you," Larsson said grudgingly.

Jordy was obviously enjoying himself. "Well, since you know all about us, you know what we want. But, seein' as how you already know *Mister* Barstow's name, you ought to know us too. Right, Wes?"

The gunman hadn't shifted his gaze from me and I felt intensely uncomfortable. He made me want to find a hole and crawl into it, waiting out the danger. No man had ever affected me so. Fear was fear, I knew, but he made my skin crawl with more than simple fear. Revulsion.

"Jordy, I got something to do," said Lacklander as he took a step toward me.

"*Wait* a minute!" Jordy stepped between us and put a hand out toward his friend. "Just sit tight, Wes. I'm gonna introduce us to these fine folks."

He turned toward me and removed his hat, holding it over his heart. Laughter bubbled in his tone. "Little lady, my name's Jordy Macklin, son of old Judge Jacob himself." He gestured with his hat toward Lacklander. "And this here's Wes Lacklander, son of no man. No woman, neither!" He hooted again, vastly amused at his own wit.

Lacklander had not removed his eyes from my face. "Jordy shut your lyin' mouth."

I nearly shivered. He spoke calmly, softly, not at all perturbed by Macklin. I wanted to cry out that he was sick, crazy in the head, but I was too afraid.

Jordy stilled his laughter, sobering abruptly. "Ain't it right we should know her name, too? Ain't it only mannerly?" He grinned provocatively at me. "Tell me your name, little lady."

"No."

His brows shot up. "No? You say 'no' to me?"

"There's no need for it. I didn't want to know yours; I won't trouble you with mine."

He hooted again, biting off a hunk of licorice. His eyes rested on me curiously a moment. He returned the feathered hat to his head.

"Little lady, I'm only bein' polite to you. Can't you do the same for me?"

I swallowed uncomfortably, oddly dedicated to my defiance. At least it hid the fear a little. "There's no manners in men like you. I don't expect any. And I intend on giving you none."

Lacklander's pale eyes gleamed. He smiled strangely and spoke in that husky, deep tone that chilled my spine. "She's got spunk, Jordy. I like that. Always have." His smile grew. "It makes it mean a lot more to me." His voice dropped to a silken whisper. "Ladies with fire are fun to put out."

I backed up a step involuntarily and saw the pleasure come into Lacklander's eyes. He followed me up a single step, and suddenly Jordy was standing between us.

"Wes, you want some sport—get it at the end of the street where we saw the soiled doves."

"I've got a woman for sport right here, Jordy, and it's been a long ride."

Macklin glanced over a shoulder and saw my bloodless face. He stepped backward until he stood next to me, then reached out and tugged my braid. It hurt but I said nothing, hoping he might tire of the amusement. I didn't like the smell in the air. Some unsettled business was churning beneath the surface of the encounter.

"Wes, she ain't hardly what I'd call a woman. And green as the grass of Colorado, I'll bet. The ones at the end of the street are all broke in already—give you a better time."

"You know how I like my times, Jordy. She'll do."

Jordy tugged my braid again and this time I jerked it out of his hand, glaring at him furiously. My reaction made him laugh, loudly and brightly.

Lacklander's eyes shone. "She didn't like that. It hurt."

A new note entered his voice, one that jerked my attention to him and made me suck in a breath. His eyes had paled oddly, as if they had somehow turned inwards. I felt like the air around me was sizzling; the store was full up with the smell of fear and demand.

"Wes," Jordy said quietly, "she ain't like that. She ain't like the kind you mean."

"She's a woman, ain't she?"

I knew something had changed, shifting the atmosphere. Jordy wasn't fooling with me anymore; he appeared to be protecting me against Lacklander. I didn't like it one bit, but things had gone far past me. Jordy, weirdly, was trying to put his friend off.

"She ain't rightly a woman, Wes. Leastaways, not yet. She's still got some growin' to do. Roundin' out."

Lacklander put up a hand and brushed away the beading of sweat on his upper lip. His eyes never once moved from me. The husky, velvet tone slid across the store once more.

"It don't matter, Jordy. I'll take my pleasures as

172

I please."

"Wes, we got work to do. Matt said—"

"I don't care what Matt said." Lacklander smiled slightly, smoothing out the lash in his voice. "I'll take my own time for what I want."

Jordy shrugged. "If that's the case—I found her first. Do your lookin' elsewhere."

"Stand away from her, Jordy."

Larsson broke the odd confrontation. "Leave her be, she's done you no harm. Let her go home. Leave her be. She's a good girl."

The bell on the door jangled suddenly and a thin red-haired man came through. He was short and heavily freckled, but he moved like a man who got obeyed when he spoke. Unlike Macklin and Lacklander, he took no care of his appearance. His clothing was old and stained and he wore a little plug hat.

I saw a big bone-handled knife at his belt, and he wore beaded moccasins. His eyes were green and flat as he stared hard at Jordy.

"Matt wants to know what's keeping you."

Jordy shrugged. "We're just funnin', Rooster, that's all. Then Wes got himself all hotted up over this girl, and you know what happens when he does that."

The man's green eyes flicked to Lacklander and I saw loathing enter them, but it was gone so fast I couldn't be certain I'd really seen it.

Lacklander was unconcerned by the interruption. But at least it got him to shift his stare from me to the red-haired man.

173

"Matt wants business taken care of first, Wes, you know that. You done your asking yet?"

Lacklander shrugged, silent. Jordy scratched at his chin absently. "I was just gettin' to it, Rooster."

"Then get it done." The man looked at me without interest. "You both got time for fooling later. Matt wants first things first."

"Sure, Rooster," Jordy said amiably.

I felt safer, somehow, with the older outlaw by the door. I thought I might be able to get by him without fuss, leaving the store before anything else occurred. I glanced up at the Swede.

"Thanks, Mr. Larsson. For everything."

The poor man was white-faced and shaken, but he managed a nod. "I'll see you later, then, Lonnie. You be careful."

I stepped carefully around Jordy Macklin and moved widely by Lacklander. As I reached the door the red-haired man moved silently out of my way. I felt like thanking him for appearing when he did, but didn't. Immense relief made me shake as I stepped out of the store into fresh air.

I tucked my packet into my pocket and undid the knot at the hitch rail, hands trembling. Being so close to the Barstows had really upset me. My knees felt weak and my belly churned horribly.

Tracker growled and snarled fiercely as I started to climb up into the buckboard. I dropped back to the dirt and spun around. Jordy Macklin stepped outside the door and slouched against the wall, chewing on a licorice whip. He grinned.

"Good dog."

174

Some of my confidence came back. I was outside, my rifle was at hand, and Tracker was ready to back me up. I stared back at him, hoping my face was blank, and trying to put mocking into my tone.

"He's been taught well. He can smell the difference in folks. The bad ones always show it."

Jordy's smile widened and his eyes glinted in amusement. But there was humor lacking in his attitude. "Maybe so, little lady, but you really ought to thank me."

"What *for?*"

He shifted position and tucked the last of the licorice into his mouth. The long, yellow feather in his hatband bobbed.

"Wes is a mighty hard man to buck once he's got his mind set on something—specially if that somethin' is female. He's like a stud-horse after a mare in heat—only the mare don't always have to be in heat. Understand? If I was you, I wouldn't want to tangle with him. He could've made some rough trouble for you, had I not stepped in. His kind of trouble gets girls like you hurt, missy. You're lucky I took your side."

"I had the idea your friend, Rooster Gibbs, kept Lacklander from doing anything."

He straightened, no longer smiling. "Rooster Gibbs wouldn't give a damn if Lacklander took you out in the street. He just had business—a message from Matt. That's all he had on his mind."

"I suppose *you* only had my *safety* in mind."

He slouched against the wall again, studying me, playing with the tie-strings of his hat. He

175

smiled slowly.

"Oh—maybe a little more than safety on my mind."

I tried to relax my stiffened joints. I wanted to leave, but refused to turn my back on him now. If he wanted to provoke me, I'd show him I knew how to play.

"Tell me something."

Jordy quirked an eyebrow, grinning evilly. "Anything for *you*."

I ignored his tone. "What's a gang like the Barstows doing in Ridgely? There's nothing for you here."

"Ain't you heard? Matt's brother, Ben, got himself hung a few weeks back, all on account of some ignorant cuss who decided to be a hero and testify against him." He shook his head dramatically. "Matt Barstow ain't a man to cross concernin' *anything*, least of all the man who got his kid brother killed. He's out for blood, plain and simple."

"But why come *here*?"

"Because Matt put a bullet in the witness when we was chasin' him. He got away, but a man don't go far with a bullet in him. We're checkin' the lay of the land."

I tried to sound innocently curious. "What—what would you do if you caught him?"

"Kill him. What the hell else would we want him for?"

"Oh."

His eyes were very sharp. "You seen any strangers hereabouts?"

176

I shrugged elaborately. "I don't come to town much. A lot of strangers come and go, and I never see them."

"You wouldn't lie to me, would you?"

My belly fluttered. "Why would I lie to you?"

His eyes narrowed. "Lot of people lie. You one of 'em?"

"No." I turned and climbed into the buckboard, done with my game-playing. He was too dangerous.

Jordy took a step forward, pushing off the storefront as if to stop me. Tracker lunged at him and I had to haul him back into the buckboard before he landed in the dirt. Jordy took the hint and stayed where he was, casually rocking on his heels. The spurs rolled and chinked.

"Good dog."

I looked at him a moment later, trying to read his benign expression, but gave it up. I slapped the reins down on the mare's back to send her off, then jerked her back. Noise had erupted from Mick's saloon. Tracker hackled up and everyone in the street and on the boardwalks stopped to see what the ruckus was.

It was Rainmaker. The old man had been tossed into the street through the batwing doors of the saloon, and now he struggled to his feet. Pitifully he tried to brush himself off, wavering and weaving. He nearly fell as he carefully placed the stovepipe hat back on his head.

A man pushed through the batwings as Rainmaker swayed in the street. He strode out onto the boardwalk and stared out at Rainmaker. His voice was loud and harsh, carrying easily.

"Old man, I told you to do your begging elsewhere. Not where there's decent men drinking."

Rainmaker remained in the street, but put out a trembling hand toward the man. "Please, mister—give me a drink. All's I want's a drink—I'll do something for you."

"*Do* something for me?"

I heard Jordy chuckle behind me. "Teach the old drunk a lesson, Matt."

I was suddenly afraid for Rainmaker. Matt Barstow was capable of anything.

"I told you to get out of my sight, old man. I hate the smell of you. It fouls the air I breathe."

"Please, mister—just a drink?"

Oddly enough, Matt Barstow only stared disgustedly out at the old man, then turned to go back inside. I started to heave a sigh of relief, but caught it back as Rainmaker stumbled after the outlaw.

He nearly fell as he stepped up on the boardwalk. He reached out a grasping hand that landed on Barstow's broad, black-jacketed back.

Barstow spun and I heard the gunshot. Rainmaker stumbled backward, off the boardwalk, falling brokenly in the dust on his back. His battered stovepipe rolled away and stopped. There was no movement.

It wasn't until the outlaw went back into the saloon that anyone had grit enough to do anything. They crowded around Rainmaker. We had no doctor in Ridgely, but I think everyone knew there was no need.

"No more beggin' for him," said Jordy.

A growing emptiness spread through me as I

clucked to the mare and sent her out. I was beyond fear now, fully realizing my precarious position.

If Matt Barstow could so easily shoot and kill a harmless old drunk, what would he do to the girl knowingly hiding the witness he wanted?

Toby would have to leave.

Chapter Eleven

The buckboard rattled over the ground as I signaled the mare to trot out smartly. I felt as if I might jerk myself to pieces, but that was the last thing on my mind.

First the Barstows would look all through town, then—finding nothing—would turn to the farms. I had no place suitable for hiding a man, and I figured the gang might tear the whole place apart if they thought there was a chance I was hiding the man they sought.

Toby's safety, not his pride, was foremost in my mind. He would have to leave me to face them alone.

He stood in the open doorway as I drove into the yard. He grinned brightly and stepped out to welcome me home, expecting my answer to his proposal. I climbed down from the buckboard and loosed the hound.

"Toby, they're here. In town."

Color fled from his face. "The Barstows?"

I nodded, shoving hair out of my face. "We haven't got much time. You unhitch the mare; I'll pack some food."

He caught my arm as I started past and swung me around. "Wait a minute! What are you saying?"

"You have to go." I stared into his incredulous face. "Toby, they'll come *here* when they don't find you in town. You must leave now, while there's time."

"I'm not going anywhere!" he exclaimed. "And leave you here alone? Don't be a fool!"

I gritted my teeth. *"You're* the fool if you stay!"

His hand tightened on my arm. "I'm not going anywhere."

"Toby!"

"I won't run from them."

Desperation clogged my voice. "You did once!"

He released me and stared at me, coloring. "Once. Before. But I won't do it again."

I pleaded with him. Me—who never pleaded with anyone. "Toby, please—you have to go. These aren't men you can run a bluff against. I've got no place to hide you."

"I don't intend to hide." He reached out and grabbed both my arms, holding me in one place. "What kind of a man would I be if I left you here to face them?"

"A live one."

"You said once I never stood my own ground— that I always ran out on things I didn't like. This time I won't, understand? I'm staying here with you."

I was so frustrated I banged at him with my hands, trying to free my arms. "Dead heroes don't mean a damned thing to me! They'll kill you if they find you!"

His eyes searched mine. "Don't you see? I'll take my stand against them. I'll do whatever I have to do. I've never done it before—now is a good time to start."

"And you'll be killed for it!" I cried bitterly.

His voice dropped to softness. "You can't handle them by yourself. No matter how stubborn you are. At least with me it means two of us against them."

"It means two graves," I said numbly. "No more than that."

He released my arms, staring at me in dawning pain. "You want me to run away. You."

"You *have* to! You're no coward, I know that. But it's pure foolishness if you stay."

"Lonnie . . ."

Suddenly I fell on a new approach. "Toby—listen to me. If they find you here they might kill *me* for hiding you and lying to them. If you go now, and they find no one, they'll leave."

"They could kill you on a whim."

I swallowed, recalling Rainmaker's sudden end. "I know. But I think they'll be in too much of a hurry to do it. And I'm only a girl. I'm no threat."

His face was blank as he stared at me, but I had learned to read his eyes. He was hurting, and I'd done it to him. I watched the conflict in his eyes and wished I could take it back.

"Lonnie—is this the only reason you want me to leave?"

"Oh, Toby."

He heard the horrified anguish in my voice. Wordlessly he reached out and pulled me into his arms, holding me against his chest. I felt safe and secure and comfortable, and for a moment I pushed away thoughts of the Barstows and the danger they brought.

"More than anything, Toby, I want you to stay. I'm no good at telling you, but it's a fact. I want you alive and safe so you can come back when things are done." I pressed my head against his chest, wrapping my arms around his waist. "If you stayed and they killed you—well, it would destroy me. I couldn't face losing someone I loved all over again."

He laughed softly. "You—who never admit emotions to anyone—admit to *loving* me?"

I took in a deep, trembling breath, knowing the time was slipping away, knowing I had to tell him.

"Well, if love is caring enough for someone to change a part of yourself, and caring enough to want them to share what you have, and being willing to share a whole life with them—well, yes. I love you."

I heard and felt him let out a long breath. His arms were tight around me. "You have no idea how you've made me feel."

"Stop feeling it and leave," I said sharply, embarrassed by my words though I meant each one. "I refuse to see you dead."

He pushed me away and stared at me, smiling crookedly. "You're about as romantic as a fence post."

"Toby—"

"I know." He tugged gently at my braid. "You're right about what they might do to you if they found me here. I'll go. I hate it, but I'll go."

I sighed, relieved. "I'll be fine. I can take care of myself. Even you have to admit that."

He smiled quickly and nodded, but his eyes were far from happy. He pulled me back against his chest. "That's so, Lonnie Ryan, but I care too much to shrug away my worries. You can't take that from me."

"I won't try." I stepped away from him. "Will you *go*? There's no telling when they might show up. I want you as far from here as that mare can take you."

"Not the mare. You need her."

"No," I said, rushing my words as my anxiety rose. "There's no reason for me to go anywhere for a while. The saddle and bridle are in the shed; you rub her down, grain her, water her. I'll pack the things you need."

Before he could launch another protest I was off for the house, running to gather supplies for him. Cans of beans, vegetables and other edibles went into an old flour sack, and I added a small bag of coffee too. I ran down to the springhouse and sawed off chunks of venison, ham and beef. A double handful of jerky went in as well.

I found my pa's old canteen, extra mug and a coffeepot, and dumped a plate and utensils into the sack. Now I needed to get him a bedroll and extra clothes.

I stripped Toby's bed of quilt and sheets, spreading them on the floor. I put a change of my pa's clothes in the middle and added a big canvas coat he'd worn. I tied the rolled bundle up as small as I could and hurried outside.

Toby cinched the mare and dropped the stirrup down. I halted abruptly, suddenly overwhelmed with the realization that he was going. Here I'd finally settled on having a man for myself, and now he was going away. Because I told him to.

Toby looked at me starkly a moment, as if he felt the same things, then led the mare to me slowly. I handed everything over to him and he tied them to the saddle. When he was done he stopped, leaning against the mare's side as if asking her support. I stared down at the ground and watched my toes make idle prints in the dust.

Tracker sat at my left side, waiting for the word he could go with Toby. To the hound a ride was a pleasureful thing, for he'd gone often with my pa, but I wouldn't let him go this time. I needed him.

Patch came trotting through the dust and headed straight for Toby, then came to me instead to avoid the mare. He wound around my ankles and under Tracker's low-slung head, talking up a storm.

Toby pushed off the mare and turned to me. I summoned up a weak smile. "You've got everything you need."

"Yes."

"You should have food enough for a little bit."

"Oh God, Lonnie, I don't want to go," he said in a groaning voice.

"You said you would."

"I know. I will. I just don't want to. I hate leaving you here." He grinned ruefully. "I don't suppose I could talk you into coming with me?"

I smiled wistfully. "No."

He stopped smiling and fastened me with a piercing stare. "Are you sure you'll be all right?"

"No." I had to laugh at his expression. "Toby, I've got Tracker and the rifle. That's all I need. I'll do just fine."

His eyes were anguished. "You've never faced anything like this."

"I figure I can handle it."

He nodded and sighed. "I know. You probably can. But I'll still worry."

A part of me longed to ask for help, somehow. I wanted him to stay; I wanted him to go; I wanted to be with him. Instead, I made myself sound unconcerned.

"Do your fretting elsewhere. You'd best go."

Wordlessly he stepped forward and pulled me into his arms. I clung to him like a wilted flower, despising my weakness, welcoming the depth of feeling I'd denied so long. I was a woman after all, with a woman's longing for a man. And he was a man willing to let me be myself.

At last he released me and stepped back, but I refused to meet his eyes. If I did he's see the anguish sweeping into my soul and the loneliness creeping back in, and he'd never go.

"Please go," I whispered hollowly.

He mounted and gathered up the reins. The mare arched her neck and bobbed her nose, snorting. She seemed a little snuffy, but I figured I owed it to her. She'd been nothing but a plow horse and harness animal for two years.

Toby drew his fingers down the side of her neck soothingly and spoke a gentle word, quieting her. He stared down at me longingly, but I found myself speechless.

"Goodbye, Lonnie."

Still I said nothing. Abruptly he set heels to the mare and spun her, putting her toward the road. It wasn't until they crested the rise that I sucked in enough wind to cry out.

"Toby!"

He halted the mare quickly and turned back, features shadowed and indistinct. I wanted to tell him to come back, stay with me, face the Barstows next to me—but I couldn't. I lifted my arm in a stiff wave.

"Goodbye!"

He answered with a wave, then he and the mare dropped below the rise and disappeared.

Tracker pressed against my leg, whining. I dropped my hand to his head and stroked it, seeking solace in the silk of his skin.

The hound lifted his muzzle and licked at my hand. I glanced down at him blindly, then dropped to kneel with him, cradling his speckled head in my hands. His brown eyes were incredibly deep.

"I know, Tracker. I'll miss him too."

Chapter Twelve

I woke with the haunted feeling of something gone wrong. As I lay stiffly in bed, sensing odd apprehension and denial, I recalled Toby's departure. A desolate loneliness swept in like a summer storm across the plains.

Yet once the realization of his leave-taking faded to a dull ache, I found I was still aware of a sensation of impending trouble. I hadn't dreamed, but something had me spooked.

As I dressed I wondered if some sort of second sight were telling me Toby was hurt, maybe dead. I flung open the front door and stared across the dirt yard to the road. I couldn't put a finger on my prickles.

Tracker wasn't by the door greeting me as he did nearly every morning, but I couldn't use that as my excuse. He slept outside, and often chased off after an intriguing scent. As I turned back to the kitchen I heard his deep, ringing bay, and went out to see what he wanted.

He loped in from the cornfield, whining, then dashed off to the lean-to. I followed, worried.

Princess and the calf were gone. I found the broken

piece of tie-rope and realized it had broken easily with pressure from the cow. It was frayed badly, and I had not thought to replace it.

I turned to Tracker and saw his eager look, ears pricked, tail waving. I nodded at him. "Go find her. Seek, Tracker."

He bounded off and I hurried after him. I doubted the cow was in trouble, but the calf was so young it wouldn't take much to trip her up.

I found them at the far end of the cornfield, safe and eating well. Of course. Princess was a glutton and much preferred tender young leaves and corn over the feed I gave her. The calf was with her, nosing the stalks curiously, too young to appreciate such food. I checked her over for hurts, but she was fine.

Princess was not particularly enamored of returning to the lean-to. No amount of tugging on the rope budged her. I threatened all sorts of dire consequences if she continued her rebellion, but she only gazed at me with the stupid, placid look cows have. I gave up.

"Listen, lady, we're going back," I told her firmly. "There's perfectly good feed for you waiting back there, and I need this crop for myself. There's more than one way to skin a cat. Or, for that matter, move a balky cow."

I picked up the calf and staggered down the hill. I laughed as I heard the cow's worried bawl, and a moment later she came with great alacrity. I nearly broke my back, but I got Princess and the calf safely to the lean-to.

As I milked the cow, muttering threats of retribution, I realized my feeling of wrongness had abated. I relaxed, grateful for the relief. My appetite came in with a rush and I recalled I had yet to eat breakfast.

Cooking for one was downright depressing. I began to regret sending Toby off. I'd done nothing but pine like a lovesick girl the evening before, curled in the rocker, and now I missed his bright talk and laughter at breakfast.

Tracker sounded off without warning outside the house, loud and threatening. I could not mistake his tone. My belly turned over sickeningly as I identified his trouble bark. What now?

I ran to the pegs and grabbed the rifle down. Then I moved out the doorway and brought the gun to my shoulder, planting my feet solidly in the dust.

Goosebumps rose on my legs and arms as I stared out at my visitors, and I realized all my fine talk of courage and defiance was about to be tested. And I had no idea if I could live up to my own expectations.

They lined up before me, strung out from one end of the small yard to the other. No one spoke, and I thought fleetingly I must make an odd sight: a lone girl with a rifle to her shoulder.

I stood my ground, acknowledging the dawning conviction within myself. I was prepared to shoot. I had at last come up against the question and I knew my words to Toby were not just bluff.

I wondered if I would kill a man that day.

Jordy Macklin looked astonished, but his expression faded into a wide, dimpled grin. He was amused by the whole matter, staring at me with laughter in his glinting eyes.

Wes Lacklander did not look amused. He did not look stunned. He looked instantly and sharply interested. I felt his pale blue eyes fastened on me in that sickening stare, and the revulsion I felt for him trickled in again.

He smiled faintly and a flush came up in his fine face. I swallowed heavily in an attempt to wash down the bitter taste in my throat. I knew him, knew him well. The man was death on horseback, and he filled my yard with raw and naked violence.

I wrenched my eyes from his face, hoping to stave off the panic edging at my mind. I could not afford to scare myself.

Rooster Gibbs sat his buckskin horse calmly, uninterested in much at all, I thought. I could barely see the flat green eyes beneath the curled brim of his plug hat, but I was very aware of his silence.

Matt Barstow sat astride a big sorrel stallion, a fidgety stud-horse that stomped in the dust. Like Lacklander, Barstow wore a black frock coat. The tails were blown back from the ride and his holstered gun shone plainly in the sun.

Rainmaker, I thought sickeningly. Poor old Rainmaker. Was I next?

He had a dark and sullen face, brooding, and carried glittering intensity in small, deep-set black eyes. His mouth was mostly hidden by a heavy mustache and his nose was flattened as if broken once or twice. He frowned down at me and I knew at once he demanded absolute obedience.

He was not surprised at the reception I gave them, or else he didn't care. More likely the latter, I thought. I wondered absently if he ever expressed any emotions other than hatred and the willingness to kill.

"You have met him at last, my girl," I whispered within my mind, "and you have seen him. He is a man you cannot fool. He is more than you ever considered."

I shivered and felt all of my high pride and arrogance trickle away like sand through an hourglass. But I dredged up something. I realized false courage still might serve. It was all I had left.

He glanced to his right and I saw an ugly scar curving from behind his left ear to his jaw. His eyes lanced into me again as he turned back, edging his horse forward a single step.

"Don't," I said softly, settling the rifle on him. Tracker growled and hackled at my left, begging a fight. He smelled death in the air as well as I did, perhaps better.

He looked me over sharply but halted his horse just the same. His hands rested over the saddle horn, holding the reins loosely as a longtime horseman does. His fingers looked thick and strong and I didn't figure he considered me much of a threat.

"You know me, missy?" His tone, low-pitched and gruff, ground into me. I recognized the quality he had used with Rainmaker.

"I know you by the men with you. I know because I saw you shoot down a harmless old man in cold blood."

A flicker passed through his black eyes. "So you saw that, did you?"

"Along with the rest of the town."

"Then you know I mean what I say, missy."

Jordy laughed. "She's the little lady Wes had the itches over yesterday." He paused. "Still does, by the

192

look of him."

I wrenched my eyes to Lacklander and saw the intensity in his face. He spoke in a cool, silken drawl that belied the tension of his body. "It won't take long, Matt. You can search the farm while I keep her occupied."

Barstow's heavy voice was sharp. "Set your horse, Wes, and shut up. There's no need for that yet."

The gunfighter seemed unperturbed. *"I've* got a need."

Jordy chuckled, amused by Lacklander's desire, but it seemed there was no threat to me after all. Barstow had made his feelings known, and his control of the others was absolute.

Matt Barstow appeared to be reading me, judging me to find out what kind of person I might be and if I meant much in my threatening posture. Suddenly he had made up his mind.

"Missy, I got no quarrel with you. There's no need for that rifle."

"I got a need," I said, purposely mimicking Lacklander.

Jordy laughed. *"If* you can use it."

"I can use it, Mr. Macklin—just try me and see."

He opened his mouth to say something back, but Barstow lifted a silencing hand. "Jordy, enough."

The youngest outlaw faded back within himself, but the expectant grin still creased his face.

Barstow stabbed me with a glare. "Missy, this ain't your business. I'll speak with your pa."

I felt creeping fear in my belly. "He ain't here."

His eyes narrowed. "Then your ma."

"She ain't here, either. Do your dealing with me."

Jordy made a soft exclamation. "She's alone, Matt. She was yesterday in town, and now. I'll bet she ain't got a soul here with her. Ever."

Barstow's eyes glittered. "All right, missy, I'll do my talkin' with you. You know why we've come?"

"I know. The whole town knows."

"You got any objections if my boys take a look around your place?"

"Lots of them. None of you will search my farm."

"You hiding somebody out here, missy?" he asked softly, ominously. "A wounded man, running from something?"

"I'm hiding no one."

His mustache moved. "Then you won't mind if we take a look around."

"I mind."

He tried a new approach. "I'd like to know your reasons, missy."

"Shall we just say I don't much like folks nosing around my place?" I tried to smile at him defiantly. "Least of all men like you. Ride on out of here, Matt Barstow. Now."

His voice dropped to a grinding whisper. "I don't let anyone talk to me like that, missy, not even a little gal like you."

"Then I'll repeat it. Ride out of here."

Barstow made an abrupt movement to step off his horse. Tracker snarled and leaped for the man, smelling blood. I saw the fury in the outlaw's eyes as he shifted back into his saddle.

"I'll shoot him, missy."

"Do it and you're a dead man for certain. Tracker, stay!"

194

I breathed a little easier as the hound returned to my side. I knew my position was precarious, for any of them could kill Tracker, disarm me and get their way, but I refused to give in. Not yet.

"Missy, you ever shot a man before?" Barstow growled.

I swallowed back my fear. "Never had any call to. I might now, though, if you step off that horse."

"You think you could shoot a man? Shoot to kill?"

Unbidden, the thought came to my mind that the subject had been very popular lately. First Dan Michael Loggins asked me, then Toby, now Barstow. And I'd asked it, too. I stared at the outlaw.

"I think I could, Mr. Barstow."

His brows drew down. "If you were lucky enough to get a shot off, gal—my men would see to it you were dead the next second."

Somehow I managed to squeeze out a smile and put a mocking tone in my voice. "Ah—but then you'd be dead too, wouldn't you? I'm no fool. You kill a snake by cutting its head off. I'll kill the Barstow snake by shooting you, Matt Barstow."

Jordy laughed. "She's got a mouth on her, ain't she?"

"Shut up!" Barstow snapped, glaring at me. "Missy, you're in my way."

"You'll go down with me. I promise. I'm no hero, but it might be worth dying if I took you with me."

He smiled grimly. "Think what you like, missy, but you're far from able. Rooster Gibbs, over there, is real good with that knife of his. He could draw it with you never knowing, and pin you before you got a shot off."

I sucked in a breath and bluffed with all my heart. "Then tell him to do it. It won't get you a thing. No one is hiding here."

"Then let us look around. We'll leave peaceable— *if* there's no one here, like you say."

"I don't like my home looked over by a bunch of scavengers."

He was dark-faced and ugly. "Missy, you're pushing my patience. You're only making me think you're lying about nobody being here."

He had a point. "All right. Your men can look. *You* stay on your horse. I'll keep an eye and my rifle on you while they look around. I don't exactly trust your kind."

"Missy—"

"Then shoot me now."

Jordy silently drew his gun and aimed it at me, playing with the hammer. I stared at him and saw the gleam of laughter in his eyes and the dimples of his smile.

"Little lady, it wouldn't be hard."

"You'd never do it," I told him flatly. "Not you."

It surprised him. "Why not?"

"You," I said softly, "think all this is funny. Killing me would ruin your fun."

After a moment he nodded, still grinning. "So it would. Well, I reckon I won't. You've won my heart, little lady."

Barstow sighed heavily. "All right, missy, we'll do it your way." He glanced at his men. "You three take a look around—a *good* look. I'll do what missy, here, says. After all, she is the one with the gun."

"I think she's spunky enough to use it." Jordy

196

laughed and started to swing down from his horse.

Tracker jumped for him. Jordy thought better of it and stayed in the saddle.

"Call off your dog," Barstow ordered.

I did so, realizing I was vulnerable once the men were on the ground. But there was nothing I could do, save shooting Matt Barstow and dying myself. I preferred to leave that until there was no other way.

The men dismounted and spread out, moving rapidly. I watched Barstow watching me. His little, black eyes chilled me to the bone, but I found some strength in my rifle and the hound at my side. I gritted my teeth so hard I feared they'd crumble in my mouth.

Gibbs came out of the lean-to and went toward the river. I knew he'd find the springhouse, but it didn't worry me. Toby, thank God, was not there.

An angry yowl came from the house and a moment later Patch flew out like his tail was on fire. He streaked away, yelling at the top of his lungs. It made me furious Lacklander and Jordy would treat my cat that way, but I could do nothing. My hands were tied.

Jordy stepped into the doorway. "Matt, there's no one here."

"You sure?"

"Yeah. Wes couldn't find nothin' either. If she'd hidin' anyone, she's got him stashed away in a spot we can't find."

Barstow's stare shifted to me. "You got anyone hid away somewhere, missy?"

"You had your look around, Barstow. You and your men can ride out of here."

"You act like you know something more, missy."

"All I know is if you don't get off my land pretty quick someone might end up dead. I'm getting tired of aiming. I'd rather shoot and be done with it."

Suddenly Lacklander was behind me. I sensed more than heard him, but realized if I moved away I'd lose the advantage I had. I sighted in on Matt Barstow and drew back on the trigger.

"Wes!" Barstow shouted.

Tracker spun and went for the outlaw, forcing Lacklander to stumble back. The man cursed violently, trying to shake loose of the hound. Tracker had latched onto his right wrist, and he could not draw his gun.

"Wes! Back off—*now!*" Barstow shouted, then pointed a finger at me. "Missy, call the dog off!"

As I did I heard Lacklander cursing up one side and down the other. Tracker still growled, longing to finish the job.

Lacklander moved to his horse, wrapping his bleeding wrist in a bandanna. I hoped Tracker had broken it.

Gibbs was back, joining the confrontation silently. He watched it all with expressionless eyes, mounting his buckskin horse fluidly.

Jordy crossed the yard behind me, giving me a wide berth. I heard him chuckle as he went. Tracker fell back in at my side, his low growl rising as Jordy walked by.

"Good dog," he said.

He swung up on his horse, laughing openly at Lacklander as the gunfighter mounted his own carefully, guarding his wrist.

"Well, Wes, looks like you finally come up against

a lady bent on avoidin' your considerable charms. That dog lit into you quicker than a rattler!"

"Jordy, hold your tongue before I cut it out!" Lacklander lashed back.

"Enough!" Barstow snapped, still staring at me.

Jordy frowned, puzzled. "Wait a minute." He looked from me to the lean-to and back, beginning to smile. He rode over to the lean-to purposefully.

Lacklander's angry tone was gone now as he called to his partner. "Jordy, you're holding us up."

Barstow grunted. "Let him have his look, Wes. He might find something."

A moment later the youngest outlaw was back, slouched in the saddle, grinning at me lazily.

"Jordy?" asked Barstow.

"Well, Matt, yesterday in town this sweet little lady had a brown mare hitched to her buckboard. There's only a cow and calf in the shed."

I felt their eyes on me. Chill washed through me and I know I paled before them, showing guilt. I licked my lips as Barstow spoke more coldly and deadly than before.

"Suppose you tell us where your horse got to."

I shrugged. "She died on me yesterday. I had a neighbor come out and drag her away so she wouldn't bring sickness down on me. Go ask in town if you don't believe me. Abner Barton, the blacksmith."

Jordy laughed. "Why wouldn't we believe you, little lady?"

Lacklander's eyes were the curious pale blue that frightened me. His tone was silken again, soft and menacing. "I'll get the truth from her. I'll make her talk. Let *me*."

"Missy, you lie to me and you'll pay the price for it," Barstow said flatly.

"I don't doubt it."

"You're too young to die, missy, but it won't stop me."

"I don't expect much of anything might stop *you* from killing. Unless maybe a hanging rope."

I saw at once my mention of the execution had done more to set the man against me than anything I'd said or done before.

"My brother got himself hung on account of some lying witness who said he saw Ben shoot a buffalo hunter," he hissed. "I tend to hold such things against those who had a part in it. Nothing is going to stop me finding that man. Not even a slip of a girl like you. I want you to understand that before you stand against me."

"I'm standing against you now. Your witness ain't here. Now, leave."

He studied me a long moment. It stretched even longer by the hard look in his eyes. I knew it might go either way; he might kill me or leave me alone.

"Missy, I give you credit for some spunk and smarts, not to mention a tongue like the devil, but I hear you lied to me and I'll be back. Understand?"

"I hear you."

Barstow glanced at the others. "Let's go." He wheeled his horse and rode away.

Rooster Gibbs fell in behind Barstow, but Wes Lacklander and Jordy Macklin stood their ground a moment longer. Each looked me over his own way.

Lacklander followed Gibbs and Barstow after

staring at me with white-faced, pale-eyed intensity. Jordy hung back and resettled his hat, grinning at me companionably. I kept the rifle pointed at him since he was the only one left, but it didn't seem to bother him at all.

Jordy spurred his horse, then abruptly reined it to a crow-hopping standstill. He hooted.

"Yes, *sir!* You are one spunky little lady!"

He wheeled his fretting horse and raced after the others.

I took the rifle down from my shoulder and very carefully laid it in the dust as I sank to the ground. I was incapable of remaining upright a moment longer. I shook horribly and felt cold, sickened.

Tracker came close and nosed at me, licking my face. All I could do was wrap my arms around him and hug him, kneeling in the dirt.

Chapter Thirteen

Eventually my heart slowed its heavy pounding, my goosebumps and shivers faded away, and the terrible trembling lessened. I could breathe normally again. I felt weak, washed out, a shadow of the person I'd always thought myself to be.

Princess got me to my feet again. She bawled loudly from the lean-to, so I hastened to see her problem. Tracker bounded ahead of me as I gathered up the rifle and ran.

There was nothing wrong with the cow. She stood where I tied her, perfectly safe. I stared at her, puzzled, for she wasn't a vociferous animal. She tugged repeatedly at the rope, bawling, stretching her head toward a pile of hay and straw on the far side of the lean-to.

Baffled, I went over to it and nearly vomited.

The heifer calf lay stretched on her side, one wide-open eye gazing blindly at the roof. Her throat had been cut.

I fell to my knees by the little calf, reaching blankly out to touch her soft, ginger-colored coat. The sweetly sickening smell of blood commingled with the scent of hay and straw, and I gagged against the stench. Tracker backed hastily away from the sodden mess of blood-soaked litter, but Princess bawled and tugged at her rope, wanting to reach her calf.

The shock of it kept me from losing my senses altogether. I was already badly shaken by my confrontation with the Barstows; I feared finding my calf butchered might drive me back into the shell I'd erected two years ago. It didn't. I kept tears at bay by using what store of strength I had left.

I buried the calf in the trees across the road, far enough away so that if scavenger animals came they wouldn't stray near the house. The whole time I dug the grave I heard Princess calling from the lean-to. Words work with people, I thought bitterly, but how do you tell a cow of the death of her young?

Rooster Gibbs. I decided on him as I walked slowly back to the house. The thin, little, red-haired, green-eyed man who hardly said a word. His doing. Here I'd named him the least dangerous of them all because of his silence and his timely interruption in Larsson's store. Gibbs of the long-bladed, bone-handled butcher's knife.

I washed off at the well and went into the house in poor spirits. As I stepped inside I halted abruptly. An overwhelming feeling of surrender engulfed me.

The place was a shambles. Jordy Macklin and Wes Lacklander had spawned a tornado in the front room.

Everything lay piled in the center of the room. Clothing, bedding, my curtains, and the lacy white cloth from the round table were heaped on the rag rug. The pile was torn and dirtied beyond repair.

203

One of the lanterns had been smashed and dropped on the pile.

By the time I finished cleaning up and making repairs, dusk had come. I had no stomach for supper. With rifle in hand and Tracker by my side I did the evening chores and check of the place. I had no heart for any of it, and I longed for Toby.

Patch showed up as I readied for bed, slipping between my ankles like a wraith. I was so happy to see him I scooped him up and hugged him to my chest, ignoring his outraged complaints. He was never one for being held, but just now I needed something. When I let him down he stomped around my bed and complained loudly, then settled down to groom his mussed fur. When I crawled beneath the covers he curled next to me on the pillow, purring warmly.

I didn't sleep for a long time.

Horses came over the hill as I drew water from the well. I dropped the bucket down immediately and snatched up my rifle. Two riders came over the crest and toward the house, and I recognized Abner Barton and Elmer Tolleson.

I hushed Tracker as they came into my yard, and set the gun against the well. Barton smiled at me. "Mornin', Lonnie."

Tolleson nodded his greeting. "Lonnie."

"Mornin'," I answered. "Step down if you like."

Barton shook his head. "No time for it. We've only come by for a short visit. We wanted to check on how you're doing."

Tolleson wiped sweat from his brow with a

bandanna. He was a tall, gentle man who always spoke in a quiet voice. He still retained a touch of his Virginia accent.

"Lonnie," he said, "you know the Barstows have been in town. They've been out on the plains too, looking for that witness. Abner and I are checkin' folks to see how they stand, to see if they've been visited. We thought we should check on you first, bein' as your farm's the farthest and you're here alone."

I nodded, recalling the fear of yesterday. "I know. They've come already."

Both men were shocked. As I saw the fearful expressions on their faces and the stricken look in their eyes, I realized what I had done the day before. It brought the memory back with vivid clarity, and a sudden shiver ran down my spine.

"Lonnie!" Barton fought to keep from shouting. "They came *here?*"

"Yesterday."

Tolleson gestured to include me and the farm. "They didn't hurt you? They didn't take advantage of you bein' here alone?"

"No. No, they didn't hurt me. They only looked around."

The blacksmith sounded normal again, but curious. "How did you hold them off? They tore apart Ed Hanley's storage shed. And *you* saw Matt Barstow kill Rainmaker. How could you stand against a man like that?"

"I kept my rifle on him. I'd have shot him if any of them had tried anything." I shrugged. "Besides, I had Tracker. He took a hunk out of Wes Lacklander's arm."

Barton's eyes sharpened. "Why did the hound jump Lacklander?"

Tolleson stared at me wide-eyed. "They *did* try to hurt you! Why else would the dog have gone at him?"

I smiled weakly. "Let's just say Lacklander got a little too close for Tracker's likes. That's why he's a good dog."

Barton shook his head. "Lonnie, you'd best come with us. We'll see you safely to town and settled in at my home. It's too dangerous for you to be out here by yourself." He forestalled my protest by raising a hand. "I *know* what you've said about it before, but I don't care. The Barstows are not men to fool with. You could have been hurt—even killed. Come with us."

I sighed. "They've already been here and gone. They won't come back. There's no reason to. I'm staying. Thanks for your offer, but there's an end to it."

Tolleson and Barton exchanged helpless glances. They knew me too well to continue with the subject. But Tolleson put in one more word.

"Lonnie-girl, you know Abner and I respect your reasons for stayin' here. But there comes a time when a *man* should do the decidin'. Please come with us."

I was exasperated. "Will no one ever let me be? Do I have to go on proving I can make a living out here? Look, the bank can't force me off my land; the Barstows can't scare me off it; and you can't invite me off it."

"Lonnie—" Barton began.

"No, I want no words from you." I sighed,

controlling the emotion in my voice. "I know you both mean well. You're good men. I thank you for your concern, but this is where I stay. I belong here. No matter what."

Tolleson knew nothing more he said could change my mind. Barton—who knew me best of all—simply accepted it. He wasn't happy with it, but he nodded his acceptance.

"Girl, you've got grit, that's for sure. More than some men I've known. But don't let your pride stand in your way if you need help. It may have helped you survive this long, but pride can also get you hurt. Lonnie, will you ask for it if you need it?"

I grinned at him. "I doubt I'll need it, now, but I'll ask for your help if I do."

Tolleson wiped his face again, surrendering. "Abner, we'd best be goin'. Other folks'll want to hear from us."

"Lonnie." Barton's voice was stern. "Look after yourself."

I smiled up at him. "I always do."

Once they were gone I went back to the well and cranked up the bucket, smiling to myself. Barton treated me like a frustrating, wayward daughter, but his concern was always there. Genuine concern from a man I considered one of the best ever born.

The Swede was another, always treating me fair and decent, always asking after me when I went in to do my trading. Tolleson too—I saw him whenever I bought hay and grain for my animals.

Maybe they'd always seen through the bitterness and harshness Toby had shown me I had. Otherwise why would three good men trouble themselves about me so?

And there was Toby. Of course his concern for me was different, but equally meaningful. More so, actually. I grinned foolishly at Tracker and held the bucket so he could reach it and lap up water.

"Well, old hound, your old friend has gone and got herself trapped pretty good. Here I've been the one saying I got no use for dreams and normal cares like loving a man, and now I'm just like all those other women. Well, maybe not exactly. Toby'll find out soon enough. I'm still me."

After supper I curled up in the rocking chair, losing myself in dreams of the future. Toby seemed to thrive on them, and maybe they might do me some good. I put the lantern on the mantle and lost myself in the shadows of the room.

Tracker jerked me from my solitary peace of mind by sounding off a savage flurry of trouble-barks outside the house. Patch bounded out of my lap as I flew from the chair and grabbed the rifle.

A gunshot rang out and I froze, stricken. I heard a cut-off yelp from the hound. My heart dropped clear to the floor, but I had no time to think.

I threw the door open, setting the rifle to my shoulder. Maybe I'd have been better off if I had hid, but it wasn't me, and I was afraid for Tracker.

There was no moon, only a thick, blanketing blackness. The lantern behind me barely reached out the door. I stared into the darkness.

A shadow loomed out of the night. It came at me. A

man, just a figure of a man, but the prickles rose. I sensed the inhuman coldness and revulsion he always dragged from the depths of my soul.

Wes Lacklander came at me out of the dark of night into the shadowed doorway. I fell back a step, staring at him in shock. Images flashed in my shuddering mind: such a cold, cold, white face—glazed and pale eyes staring—shiny, silver buttons glinting on his vest. His hands swam before my eyes as he reached out for me, teeth gleaming in a terrible triumphant smile.

"Now," he whispered in that sickening, silky tone, "now we'll see if you like it. Now I can have what I need."

I didn't think. I acted on pure instinct. I pulled the trigger and heard the shot ring out, ringing in my head, jarring the rifle stock against my shoulder.

I did it, Toby, I've shot a man.

But the man didn't die. He still came at me, reaching for me, clawing at me. He still smiled gently in the face of my terror. I cried out, frozen with the rifle clutched in my hands.

Then he fell backwards. He fell from top to bottom, as if he were collapsing bit by bit. The twisted legs sprawled in the front room while the rest of him hung out the doorway, head dragging in the dust.

Shuddering, spasmodic breaths started up in my chest as I slowly crept forward to see if he was dead. I've never before wanted a person hurt or dead, but I prayed for it.

Blood spread slowly across his black vest, dulling the silver buttons. I felt sick.

Toby, I've killed a man.

"I been wantin' to shoot that bastard for a long time. Now you gone and done it for me."

I spun around in shock. All I could do was stare woodenly at Jordy Macklin.

He grinned at me, folding his arms across his chest. His eyebrows slid up. "So now you know you had the guts to do it."

I tried to haul the rifle up to my shoulder but he only laughed at me, then grabbed it from my hands.

"It's empty, little lady. No more killin' for you tonight." He shook his head. "I really didn't think you'd manage, but you got ol' dead Wes smack in the gut. He didn't stand a chance."

"What do you want?"

Jordy set the rifle down on the table and shifted his weight enough to slouch lazily. The spurs chinked. He tugged playfully at the tie-strings of his hat, bobbing the feather. His tone was openly amused and overly friendly.

"Well now, I guess I ought to tell you about ol' Wes—seein' as how you just sent him on to Glory." He snatched off his hat and held it over his heart a moment, staring past me to the body in the door. "Wes, you have my condolences. But you deserved it, you bastard." He returned his hat and grinned at me. "You see, ol' dead Wes liked his women. So do I, but not for the same reasons. Women are for beddin', but Wes, well, he had some crazy ideas about it. He liked killin' and beddin' about the same—said they both gave him a powerful pleasure. Generally he liked to kill the ladies when he was done with 'em." He shook his head, smiling. "Ol' Wes was different. He liked to kill whenever he got the urge and the itch."

I nearly flinched as Macklin stuck out a finger, pointing at me. "The other day at the store, he got it in his head that he wanted you—pure and simple. I didn't figure he'd let it be, specially after you set that dog on him yesterday." He hooted. "When he rode out of camp tonight I had a feelin' he was comin' here, so I just followed along. Ol' Wes always was a little stupid—he never figured on you shootin'. So he came in the front. Now me—I know better. I came in a window." He gestured widely with both hands. "See there? You never even heard me."

"Why don't you take your friend and go."

Jordy put on a look of great surprise. "Wes was never my friend. Just a man to ride along with. Besides, I ain't ready to go just yet. Not till I find out if you would've been worth his time."

"Get out of here!"

Macklin removed his hat and dropped it to the table beside the rifle. His grin was trimmed to an expectant smile. I turned to run but he grabbed my braid and hung on, jerking me back. I cried out from the pain and struggled, but he dragged me into his arms. One hand slipped to the collar of my dress, ripping the cloth from my shoulder.

I kicked and I clawed and I bit but it only made him laugh. I must have hurt him once or twice because he cursed, but he was much stronger than I ever dreamed a man could be. Yet I wasn't about to give up the fight. Jordy Macklin had said I had spunk; now let him see how it served me.

211

I got my left arm free and clawed at the gun on his hip, but he slapped me forcefully on the side of my head. He hooked a boot heel around my ankles, digging the sharp spur rowel into a leg. He pulled me off my feet and bore me down on the rag rug with him on top.

I was crushed beneath his weight. As he shifted I tried to pull away frantically. He grabbed for the front of my dress again, fingers digging into me. His other hand was rough and painful on my thighs.

Again he shifted his weight, lifting slightly, and I used all my panicked strength to push upward in an effort to lunge away. A hand went around the base of my throat, throttling me. I feared he might murder me then, but he only shoved downward sharply. My head slammed against the floor.

Pain shot through me, bright and sharp. Stars and lights and colors jolted in my head. My eyes felt like they were bulging from their sockets.

I cried out once, then quite suddenly awareness slid softly away. I was conscious but stunned to utter blankness. I heard Jordy's grunt of triumph from far away.

He had tamed his little lady.

My mind detached itself from my body. I was perfectly aware of what Jordy did, but somehow my struggling spirit shielded me from complete comprehension. I could do nothing as he hurt me, purposely rough, mumbling horrid things to me. There wasn't even a spark of defiance left in me.

At last he was gone. The weight of him—the smell of him—the demand of him was gone. I heard him moving around the room but it came to me faintly. I made no effort to open my eyes or move. I lay there, finally slipping into some form of sleep.

I roused in the early dawn. The floor was hard beneath my sore, battered body. My head was packed and ringing. I licked weakly at a split lip and tasted dried blood. I put a hand to my mouth and bit a finger, forcing back the tears, the bone-shuddering sobs. Crying would do no good. Not now.

Sitting up took time. I was limp and weak as a rag doll, and as totally empty of emotions. Finally I managed to drag myself to my feet, hanging onto the table for support. I stared down at my empty rifle. Then I looked sharply to the open doorway.

Wes Lacklander's body was gone. Only blood-stains remained, soaking into the wooden floor. A man killed by my hand had been hauled off like a side of beef by an outlaw who denied calling him a friend, yet returned him to his own kind.

Summoning all the strength I'd ever had, wishing I had more, I stumbled to the doorway and braced myself against the frame. For a moment I stared dazedly at the mud in front of the door, wondering if it had rained. Then I realized it was Lacklander's blood. I shuddered violently once and looked past the drying puddle to the yard.

Tracker was there. The hound lay on his side, head stretched toward the house. He was dusty and bloody and stiffly dead.

I whimpered like a sickly animal. Then I was

213

down in the dirt by him, gathering him into my arms. A hole the size of a man's fist had torn open his chest. Lacklander had fired directly into the dog.

I pulled as much of Tracker into my lap as I could. I hugged him tightly, telling him over and over I loved him and he was a good dog. He couldn't hear me but it didn't silence me. For once my grief would show.

I rocked back and forth, hugging him, my head against his. I cried. After two years it came hard to me, tearingly harsh, and it wouldn't stop. My tears fell on him, spotting the dust in his hair.

After a while the sharp pain spent itself and I halted my rocking. I just sat there, holding onto my bluetick hound.

They found me like that. Hours later. I saw them come and I watched as they stepped off their horses. I said nothing. My eyes told them to go away and leave me with my dog, but they didn't go.

Abner Barton. The Swede, Larsson. And Elmer Tolleson. How ironic the men who had found me two years before with my murdered family should find me now with my dead dog.

They came to me, hesitant, awkward in their concern. The burly blacksmith knelt before me, looking at me with words in his eyes. I dropped my gaze to Tracker, denying the man his silent speech.

He was very gentle. "Lonnie, we'll see to your dog. I promise."

I said nothing, hugging Tracker harder as I realized they meant to take him from me.

Larsson whispered a soft exclamation to himself in Swedish. I glanced up and saw Barton looking at the

214

bruises all over me, made visible by my torn dress. An expression in his eyes and face made him ugly as he realized what had happened.

I wanted to run away. I wanted free of him and the others, but I couldn't move. And I had Tracker to look after.

The blacksmith put a gentle hand on my arm, then removed it hastily as I flinched jerkily, uncontrollably. I hung on all the harder to my hound.

"Lonnie, please—let us tend to him for you. You can't sit here like this. There's no help for the dog now. He's dead. Lonnie, come on, we'll take care of him."

Barton's voice was soft and soothing. I stared hard at him to make certain of his meaning, and very suddenly I couldn't stand against his wishes any longer. Jordy Macklin's victory was complete. My pride and my grit were gone.

The blacksmith took my arms and drew them away from my hound. He turned his head away, speaking softly to the others.

"Olaf, take the dog. Pull him away from her while she's willing. We can bury him when we're sure she's all right."

The Swede moved in and bent over to Tracker, starting to lift him from my lap. I stiffened and reached out for him, but Barton stood up slowly, pulling me up with him. He held me against his big body as if I were his own child, brawny arms gently cradling me. I stared after Tracker as the Swede settled him carefully in the dirt.

"Easy, Lonnie, it's over now," Barton said softly.

I looked into his face and saw something shining

like tears in his eyes. It struck me odd—why would a grown man like him cry? It was my dog.

Then I saw he wasn't looking at Tracker. He was looking at me. I wanted to tell him I didn't need that sort of fretting—never had—but as I opened my mouth to say it, somebody swept the earth right out from under my feet.

The darkness was sudden and surprisingly soft.

PART III

"The Farm"

Chapter Fourteen

I roused listlessly, restless. I huddled beneath the covers in lazy comfort, but something nagged at my blurry awareness. Slowly I surfaced, worn out to the bone. I felt like I'd been stomped on by a team of horses.

My eyes flew open and I stared up at the roof. I sat up in alarm, but the sudden movement plunged the room into whirling circles and I sank back, groaning in discomfort.

I remembered it all.

A step in the doorway brought my eyes wide open in quick fear. I blinked as I recognized Abner Barton's wife, Emily.

"Lonnie," she said softly, "are you fully awake?"

I nodded. "What—why am I in bed? The last I remember was your husband."

Her face was calm as she came into the bedroom. I realized I lay in the big bed in the bedroom Toby had used, not my own.

"Lonnie, you've been a little fevered the last couple of days. Nothing to worry about. You just need a little time to recover."

I looked up into her plain, kindly face. "He told you? You know—everything?"

She nodded. "Yes, Ab told me. He thought it might be best if I came here, rather than carting you into town for care." She smiled warmly. "You'll be fine. You're a strong girl, Lonnie."

I stared at her blankly, recalling in horror the look on Wes Lacklander's face and the tone of his voice as he came at me. And Jordy Macklin. I shuddered once, then lay back against the pillows.

She moved closer, watching me in concern. "It's past now. It's finished. You don't have to be afraid any longer."

All the aches and bruises woke up. I licked at my bottom lip and felt the healing ridge. I closed my eyes a moment, but opened them as I felt a cool hand touch my forehead. Mrs. Barton looked down on me with a look in her eyes that made me realize how much she and her husband truly cared.

"I'm not afraid," I told her. "There's nothing more to be afraid of. I've killed a man, and I've been—" I shivered again—"Oh—oh, my God."

She smoothed my hair back. "Cry, if you want. You've got to let it out. What you've been through is something too upsetting to ignore. You must give in to it, then let it go."

"I'm fine," I insisted shakily. I met her eyes defiantly. "Fine. I don't—I don't let anything bother me, remember?"

She sighed, accepting my sharp words. She understood better than I did.

"Where'd they bury Tracker?"

220

"Up on the hill by the cornfield, beneath the cottonwood tree."

"He'd like it there."

She twisted her hands. "I'm sorry, Lonnie. I'm sorry he's dead. I know how much you loved that dog."

"He was—he was a good dog." I heard Rainmaker's voice echo the same words in my mind, and suddenly felt horribly lost and alone. I steadied my voice with effort. "He's got no debts to pay. He died protecting me. That's the way it should be."

She hesitated, then went on. "Our redbone female just had a litter. You're more than welcome to one of the pups."

I gasped. "Oh, no. No. Thank you, but I wouldn't feel right, taking one so soon. It would be like telling Tracker he's easy to replace. It—it just wouldn't be right."

"Of course. Perhaps that's the right decision. There will be more pups later. Here, let me get something for you to eat. You're probably half-starved."

When she came in with breakfast, Patch trotted after her. He leaped onto the bed and stalked up to me, tail thrust bolt upright. I welcomed his warmth and tugged at an ear fondly. He was all I had left.

I spent the next day wrapped in the quilt, curled in the rocking chair. Lassitude had invaded my bones and I stared listlessly out the front door. I couldn't summon up enough spirit to think about much other than odd little bits and pieces.

Emily Barton, baking bread for me, seemed to sense my wandering mind. "Lonnie, Ab and the boys came over while you were sick. They tended the crops and looked after the cow. And weeded your garden, and fed the chickens." She smiled as I glanced back at her, startled. "Lonnie, did you think we wouldn't care?"

That brought pain welling within my chest. I struggled against it and finally won. "No, no, I know you do. But I don't understand it."

"It's what friends and neighbors are for."

"But I've never been very neighborly, and not much friendlier. I—I don't deserve it from people."

"Well, you've had your ghosts to fight off."

"Ghosts?"

"Lonnie, Abner and I have always understood why you wanted to stay on out here after your family was killed. It was an odd notion at the time, and we expected you'd change your mind, but you never did. And we began to see that you needed it."

"Others didn't."

"Those are the ghosts I meant." She removed a steaming loaf of bread from the oven and set it out to cool. "I don't blame you for keeping to yourself. You had every right. What was said of you and to you by those others was not kind. But a few of us understood."

"You and your husband. The Swede. Elmer Tolleson. And I'm grateful for you all."

She smiled at me brightly. "You've proved everyone wrong. Or maybe you've proved you've got the determination and pride it takes to do it. Those who don't recognize your strength are fools.''

"*Toby knows,*" I thought. *And even Loggins, I'll bet. He's a hard man to figure, but I think he knows me better than I do.*"

"Well," I told her, "maybe it's all been worth it."

"Of course it has. Want some bread?"

My stomach rumbled. "All of it."

She allowed me outdoors next morning, and I sat contentedly on the bench and watched the day. Drifting dust caught my eye and I watched the arrival. Abner Barton on his sorrel horse.

He dismounted and came up to me. His mouth was smiling but his eyes were not. "Lonnie, you look well."

"I am well."

"Last time I saw you, my wife had you bundled up in bed. I wasn't sure you recognized me."

"I didn't recognize myself."

He nodded absently, removing his hat to wipe at sweat on his brow. "I'm certainly glad to see you doing so well."

"What's your bad news?"

He froze. "Bad news?"

"Go ahead and tell me."

After a moment he smiled wryly and folded his arms against his broad chest. "I should've known. Of course you're better. You pick things out of my head before I can even speak them."

"What is it?"

He shook his head. "I came to tell my wife, not you. It's something she and I have been discussing."

"Does it concern me?"

"It concerns you."

I stared at the ground and drew lines in the dust with my toes. I hunched a shoulder and tugged my braid. "I know what you're going to say. You're going to tell me I should move to town with you."

"Do I have a reason to, Lonnie?"

I jerked my head up and stared at him. The plea no longer existed in his voice. He was calm and assured, and very puzzling.

"But—you can throw my own words back at me! You said I would be safe with your family, but I refused your offer in order to stay here. It's my own fault I got hurt."

"I would never say that to you."

"But you *could.*"

He came and sat down next to me, his bulk dwarfing me. I felt his reticence and waited, wondering what could make a man like him hate to speak. We both stared at the ground.

"Lonnie, I didn't want to tell you yet. I hadn't expected to. But since you're feeling so well—well enough to argue with me—I guess I'd better explain things."

"I think maybe you better."

He sighed. "I haven't come to ask you to move in with Emily and I. I've come to say you'll *have* to."

"What?"

"The bank has foreclosed your land. The deed has been made over to Higgins. Lonnie, the farm isn't

224

yours anymore."

I drooped on the bench. All my breath was gone. The nightmare of Lacklander and Jordy had altered my whole spirit; I hardly knew myself. Before, I would have answered back angrily and quickly. Now all I could do was think in tumbling fragments that never reached my lips in coherent speech. I had been stripped of the ability to accept troubles rationally.

Barton knew it. He put a big hand on my arm gently. "You know Emily and I want very much to provide a home for you."

"My home—my home is here."

"Lonnie—"

"How soon does Higgins want me off the place?"

Barton reached down for a rock and hurled it away. "Two weeks. He's giving you two weeks."

"Generous of him."

"You're lucky to get that long. He wanted you out yesterday. After I told him—well, I had to—he agreed to extend the deadline."

"*You told him?*"

"Not all of it, Lonnie," he said gently. "Not all of it. Just enough."

"Ridgely will say I'm even crazier, now."

"No one will ever say that!"

His fierce tone astounded me. I stared wide-eyed at him, then put a hand out to touch his arm. "No, I reckon they won't. With you to stand up for me like that."

Color rose in his big-featured face and he looked a little abashed, but proud too. "Emily and I consider you a daughter. You know that."

225

"Thanks. But I'm Ryan-born."

"I know that. I'd want it no other way. All I meant is you shouldn't feel deserted."

I saw myself sending Toby away. "No, I'm not deserted."

"I'll help you move to town when your time is up."

"I'm not coming."

"Lonnie—"

"No. I haven't changed my mind. The bank and Mr. Higgins do not get my land."

He shook his head, perplexed. "You can't fight them! Haven't you seen that it brings you nothing but sorrow and pain?"

"As much as I despise a man like banker Higgins, I still can't quite think of him as dangerous as a member of the Barstow gang. I hardly think he would be so cruel."

Barton was visibly shocked I could so easily refer to the Barstows. Yet all of it had happened. Denying it would not make it go away. It was a fact of life. My life.

"No, Lonnie, Higgins is not a Barstow, nor does he behave like one. But he does have the law on his side."

"Would he have me forced from my land?"

"Legally."

"If I stood him off, like I did the Barstows?"

His tone denied it. "Could you do that?"

He didn't believe I could. I knew better. "I would do anything to protect my land. I shot and killed a man, Mr. Barton."

"What?"

226

I realized he knew nothing of Wes Lacklander. I rose and walked away from him, staring across the land. Finally I turned and met his stunned eyes.

"I did. I killed him. Wes Lacklander. Before—before Jordy."

He was horrified. "Oh my God, my God—Lonnie . . ."

I swallowed, hugging myself. "Loggins said it wasn't easy. Not so easy as a bullet flying from a gun. He was right. It's the knowledge that hurts so much. A man's life."

"Lonnie—Loggins? Who—"

"Nothing," I said. "Nothing at all. But I killed him." I shook the memory off. "The bank doesn't scare me."

"Lonnie, I had no idea—"

"You said you would side with me."

"I have sided with you. I've argued against Higgins from the very beginning. But there comes a time when the law is right. Like now. *I* know what this place means to you, but there's nothing more to be done."

"I have no way to pay off the debt."

"And no way of raising it in two weeks."

"No. How much is it?"

"Three hundred and forty dollars."

It took my breath away. "I doubt I even have four dollars in the house. I guess Higgins knew it was a stacked deck all along."

He turned his hat in his hands, silent. I thought he was embarrassed about something. I waited, and finally he got it off his chest.

"You've never been one for charity, Lonnie, but we felt it was something we had to do."

"Who?"

Emily Barton stepped through the door and joined her husband. She sent him a glance, then spoke up before he could protest.

"He and Elmer Tolleson and Olaf Larsson got together, Lonnie, to pay your debt. They put together the money they could, but it wasn't enough. They were afraid to tell you they'd failed."

I stared open-mouthed at them both. This sort of emotion was something I'd never expected from people, certainly not the way I'd kept myself defiantly distant for so long.

"But—why?"

"Because you're special to all of us," Barton said. "We know what this farm is to you. It's your family. Now that your people are dead, the farm is your kin. It—it seemed the only thing to do."

"Your own money? To pay off my debt?" I took that back instantly. "Well, the debt Mr. Owen should've paid."

"We didn't have enough," he said hollowly. "I'm sorry."

"I wouldn't have taken it anyway. I pay my own way." I smiled sadly at him. "But I thank you for it, anyhow."

Emily Barton sighed. "Oh, Lonnie, why be so prideful? We're your friends."

"It wouldn't be right." Suddenly a thought occurred to me. "Is that why you all rode out here that day? The day—the day you found me with Tracker?"

"Yes," said the blacksmith. "We wanted to tell you what we had planned. So you'd know you weren't alone."

"Oh."

"I guess it doesn't matter. Now." He stood and put his hat back on. "I have to go. I have a horse to shoe and a plow to repair."

"The others," I said impulsively. "Tell the others I'll be in to see them soon. To thank them personally."

"I will. They'll be glad to hear you're fit and feisty again." He frowned. "I'll see about finding you a horse. I guess the Barstows stole your mare."

I felt blood drain from my face. *Toby.* Barton stared at me strangely, opening his mouth to ask something, but I spoke up quickly.

"Yes. The Barstows took the mare."

He nodded and began to turn away, then paused and glanced back. "Did the calf die? I figured your cow was healthy enough to drop a good one."

"The calf—died."

"Ah, Lonnie, it seems like you've had a bad time of it lately. But we'll see things get better for you. I promise."

I grinned at him. "I'll hold you to that."

When I was healthy enough, Emily Barton went back to her own home. I felt an odd sort of peace steal over me. Once again it was just me and my land.

I walked up to the cottonwood tree by the cornfield

and found Tracker's grave. It lay deep in shade, shadowed by sun-glimmered leaves. Spring flowers dotted the ground beneath the tree and I coaxed the blooms toward the grave, hoping they'd grow over it eventually.

I sat down by the mound and leaned against the tree. I needed desperately to find the calmness I'd felt before, the unruffled attitude I'd always faced life with. I was frightened by my inability to win back my defiance and confidence. Nothing was the same anymore. Least of all me.

It took effort to ready myself for the fight for my land. Effort, when before it had been instinct.

My mind wandered easily now. Odd images crept into my mind when I least expected it. It wasn't enough to make me fear for my sanity, but it was curious. Too many things had forced their way into my life, destroying the hard-won balance, the delicate structure I'd built in order to survive.

First Toby, bringing initial change. He had broken my guard in innocence, tearing down my defenses, robbing me of my illusions governing myself.

He had fashioned a new Lonnie, someone he cared for and who cared for herself. The new Lonnie, learning to love, had been shattered before she had grown accustomed to herself.

I'd watched harmless old Rainmaker murdered in the streets of Ridgely while others watched as well, doing nothing. We had been helpless to aid the old man. Helpless because of our own fears.

I had forced myself to send away the man I finally

admitted to loving, sending a part of me with him.

My heifer-calf was butchered, and I'd cradled my beloved hound in bruised and sore arms, hardly aware of my own battered body, feeling only a deep, abiding grief at his death.

And I had killed a man.

Chapter Fifteen

The sound of a rider coming over the hill didn't alarm me. Abner Barton came every other day to make certain I was all right, and to bring me news about the bank. So far Higgins was being quiet, solicitous, Barton said, because of what had happened. I doubted that. He was just biding his time, like a cat at a mousehole.

I knew it wasn't Barton the moment the rider topped the hill. His bulk wasn't the right size, and his horse wasn't a shiny sorrel gelding. It was a brown horse, a perky-stepping mare headed home.

I ran pell-mell out to the road. "Toby! *Toby!*"

He swung off the mare and met me at the edge of the ruts, laughing as he pulled me into his arms.

"Toby, you came back!"

"Of course I came back." He crushed me against his chest. "I said I would."

Suddenly I stiffened. I pushed against him, breaking away. I backed up a few feet and stared at him. I hugged myself with crossed arms, tightly.

"Lonnie . . ."

I shivered. "Why did you come back?"

He stared at me open-mouthed. "Lonnie—I said I would. You asked me to. Lonnie—what's wrong?"

"You can't stay."

He looked completely bewildered. "Do you still fear the Barstows? If so, you—"

"Barstows!" I cried. "What do *you* know about the Barstows?"

He took a step toward me but I backed up farther. I couldn't put a name to what ailed me; I only knew I couldn't let him stay. I knew. I was different. He wouldn't want me anymore.

"You began it all," I murmured, staring at him blankly. "You brought them."

"Lonnie!"

"Toby—I can't help it. The Barstows—"

"Are dead."

"One of them!" I cried. "Only one of them!"

"All of them," he said softly, staring at me.

"Only one," I shuddered. "Only Lacklander. Him. Just him."

He started to shake his head, then stopped. A frown came into his eyes. "Lonnie, I watched the Barstows hang last week."

"*Hang?*"

"They're dead. All of them."

"*Lacklander* didn't hang!"

Toby shook his head. "No, he died before. A few days before the posse caught the others." He stopped short. "But—how did you know?"

"*I killed him.*"

"You?"

233

"I killed him. Me." I stared at him fiercely. "You wondered if I could. Loggins said I couldn't. But I did."

"Oh, Lonnie—oh no."

"Don't touch me!"

He halted, arms falling to his sides. "But—why? I—I know killing him must have been horrible. But I understand. It had to be done. You said you could, if it had to be done. Why are you acting like this?"

"I'm not the same, Toby."

"Because you killed a man? He was an outlaw, Lonnie! A murderer."

"Not because of him! Not—not because of Lacklander."

"Then *why?*" he cried, reaching for me again.

I retreated hastily, wanting to flee. Toby moved more quickly and caught my arm, shaking me. "Stop it! You're acting half-crazy!"

I stared at him wildly, stiff in his grasp, afraid. "Toby," I said brokenly. "No man—no man will want me now. He couldn't."

"Why?"

I found I couldn't tell him. I could not find it within myself to say the words. They sickened me; I knew they'd sicken him. I could not face the look of disgust he would have on his face. Shaking, I refused to look at him.

His hand tightened on my arm. "Lonnie, you don't have to explain. I think I know."

"Do you?" I whispered miserably.

"I think—I think only a woman can truly understand the horror. But I think I know."

234

I jerked my head up and saw the pain and anger in his eyes. His fingers hurt and I winced. Abruptly he let go, staring blindly at me.

"I wish," he said in a harsh whisper, "I wish I'd been the one to trip Jordy Macklin's trap door. I wish I'd been the one to put the noose over his neck."

My mouth opened. "You know it was Jordy?"

His face was white and very taut. "He said something. In jail. He said—he said there was a girl outside of Ridgely who had had the spunk forced out of her. I just never thought—"

"You talked to Jordy?"

His gaze came back to mine. "Yes. In Clayton. When I testified."

I shook my head, completely lost. "Toby, what are you saying?"

"Let's go in the house. I'll explain it all."

He sat in the rocker. I sat on the rug at his feet. Patch wandered in and came to settle in my lap. I stroked him as Toby told me his tale.

"I holed up in a little town the Barstows had already visited. I worked as a hired hand for my keep, hoping I could get back to you pretty quick. Then I heard a posse was hot on the Barstows' trail. News came in a little later they'd been caught. I telegraphed the sheriff in Clayton, where they were in jail, that I was the man who had originally testified against Ben Barstow. I offered to again. When I got to Clayton, I found out Lacklander was already dead."

"What did you do?"

"Testified at their trial. They were sentenced to hang."

235

I swallowed. "Between the two of us, we've rid Kansas of a plague."

He nodded. "You know, up to the minute the rope snapped his neck, Jordy kept yelling about a pardon. That his father the judge would pardon him."

"Do you think he might have?"

"No. The sheriff contacted Judge Macklin to inform him of the trial, and he wired back he had no intention of attending. He said Jordy had finally caught up to the fate he'd been chasing all his life."

"He was his *son*."

"The old man disowned him before he died." Suddenly Toby grinned. "You know who I saw at the trial?"

"No."

"Dan Michael."

"Loggins was there?"

"He said he wouldn't miss it. And anyway, he ran them to ground. He was leading the posse."

"Loggins! But he's a bounty hunter."

Toby shrugged. "The deputies and sheriff of Clayton didn't hold it against him. Said they benefited from his law experience and his knowledge of the Barstows."

"So he got his wish."

Toby grinned at me. "He offered us his best wishes. When I told him we were getting married. He said he wasn't a bit surprised."

I stared at him. "We can't get married. Not now."

"Why *not?*"

"I told you. I'm not the same. What Jordy did—"

"I don't care!" he cried. His hands gripped the

rocker arms and he glared at me. "I'm sorry it happened—I'm sorry for you—but I don't care! You're still the same to me."

"But I'm not!" I said, horrified he could think so.

He slid out of the chair and knelt in front of me. "Lonnie, you are."

"How can you still want me?"

"Because I love you, Lonnie. *You*. No matter what's happened, Lonnie Ryan is still Lonnie Ryan." He caught my hands before I could pull away. "Don't turn me away. Please. You said you loved me."

Patch stood up in my lap, stretched, stared at Toby and wandered away. Both of us laughed, and then I sighed.

"All right. I still love you. And I still want you to stay."

He grinned brilliantly. "Then I will."

I sucked in a shaky breath. "We don't have much to start with. Maybe nothing."

"What do you mean?"

"Tracker's dead."

Bleakness welled in his eyes. "They killed the hound?"

"Lacklander shot him."

"Lonnie—"

"Rooster Gibbs slit the calf's throat."

"Oh God."

"I'm losing the farm."

That stopped him cold. "You're *what?*"

"The bank says it's something to do with a debt the original owner never paid. He says—this greedy man

237

Higgins—that now I owe it. I can't pay it, and now the land is his. Legally.''

"Legally, maybe, not rightfully.''

I grinned. "I knew you'd agree.''

"What can we do?''

Desolation washed in. "Nothing.''

"What's the debt?''

I told him, and he blanched. "So much.''

"Toby, I'm tired. I'm tired of fighting people off with my gun. My dog is dead and the land ain't mine anymore. I just don't have the strength anymore.''

"You can't give in!''

"No. I'll stick it out. Till the end.'' I sighed. "A whole week.''

He looked around the room bleakly. "Oh, Lonnie—if only I had some money.''

"Me too.''

Toby sighed heavily, eyes shadowed as he stared at me. He took a careful breath, and spoke just as carefully. "Then I guess—I guess we'll just have to go somewhere else.''

I gaped at him. "Go . . .''

"I know you love it here. I know it's your home. But if there's nothing we can do—Lonnie—'' he stopped and swallowed— "We'll just have to move on. Like all the others.''

"Leave?'' I warbled unsteadily. "Here?''

Pain filled his eyes, tautening his face. "I don't like it, either.''

"Oh, Toby!'' I wailed. "I don't want to leave!''

He pulled me firmly into his arms and this time I didn't back away. I clutched at him.

238

"I know, I know," he whispered against my head. "But we'll make do. You're tough and determined, and I'm willing to start carrying the load I denied so long. We'll make out. We'll go west, like all the others. Maybe California."

"But I don't want to!" I cried into his neck. "This is mine!"

He let me go and looked at me sadly. "Lonnie, you've got to realize, sometime, that you can't always have what you want."

I stared at him, anguished, and knew he was right.

I left him in the house. I was unable to coherently explain to him what leaving would do to me. I saw no way of convincing him of my need for the farm. Even with Toby, I realized my strength came from the land. Me without it, well, it wasn't me.

Tracker's grave lay shadowed beneath the tree. I stood over it, staring at the mound. My body felt heavy and my heart hurt. My eyes ached, but I refused to cry.

Old hound, you may be the best off of us all. You, at least, died doing what you had to do. This damn bank is tearing me up, and I can't do what I want. I can't fight them. Not anymore.

I hugged myself and looked up, staring bleakly across the cornfield. I knew fundamentally I remained the same, but my spirit had taken a dreadful beating. I despised myself for it, but I finally realized the futility of fighting it any longer. There was simply nothing left.

"I *could*," I said softly, "march into that bank with my rifle and place it square against banker Higgins' fat belly. I *could* tell him all about me shooting Wes Lacklander. I *could* threaten to do the same to him." I sighed. "But I won't. As much as I love this land, it ain't worth killing a man over."

I swallowed and straightened my hunched shoulders, realizing my decision was made. Toby would want to know, so I went off to tell him.

He faced me in the room, incredulous. "You've decided *what?*"

I glared at him. "You heard me. We've got nothing left—the bank owns it all. I guess even the mare goes to old Higgins, but if we leave quick enough he won't have to know. Let's start packing."

He continued to stare at me, and slowly closed his open mouth. "Now?"

"If we wait much longer, I'll take root. Then you'll never get me out of here."

Slowly a smile crept across his face. I saw a light come up in his eyes, and then he was pulling me against his chest.

"I knew it," he said. "I knew you'd do it. You'll never let anything defeat you."

"Higgins did," I told him.

He hugged me tightly. "No, I don't think he did."

I said nothing, content in his arms.

A step sounded at the open door. "A pretty sight," said Dan Michael Loggins.

I gaped at him, stunned. Toby wrenched around, turning loose of me, and grinned as he reached out his hand. Loggins strode into the room and took it, then smiled crookedly at me from beneath his mustache.

"I knew you'd figure out what you wanted, sooner or later."

He frustrated me, as always. "If you're so smart, figure out a way to save my farm."

His eyebrows slid up. "Farm?"

"Never mind," I said, angry at myself for mentioning it. It was hardly his concern.

I finally smiled at him. Loggins removed his hat and hung it on the door peg. Like before. I shook my head at him. He'd never change.

"Got any coffee?" he inquired.

"I'll make some," I said, resigned.

Toby and Loggins sat at the table, reliving the trial and hanging. I listened silently as I fixed them both something to eat. I was glad the Barstows were dead, but it gave me no particular pleasure. I was past that.

"When'll you two get hitched?" Loggins asked.

I looked at Toby and shrugged, realizing it might complicate our move. "We haven't decided."

Loggins stared at the both of us a long moment, then smiled slowly. His eyes glinted. "Don't wait too long."

Flushing badly, I glared at him. "You're despicable!"

He stared at me, astonished. "I'm *what?*"

"Despicable," said Toby, grinning. "Her mother was an educated woman."

Loggins was clearly affronted. "Well, educated or

not, it's no way for Lonnie to talk. Certainly not to a man, and one her elder at that. Particularly when it's not true.''

"*You* say," I muttered.

He sighed and shook his head sadly. "And here I'd even come all this way just to give you a piece of good news. With treatment like this, I should saddle up and ride away. Leaving you all unawares.''

"What news?" Toby asked.

"The reward, of course. For the Barstows. Part of it's yours.''

"Mine?" Toby stared at him blankly. *"Mine?"*

Loggins nodded, smiling benevolently. "All posse members got a share. It was a mighty substantial reward, I must say. Of course I'd wanted it for myself, but since I had a posse with me, it was only fair it got parceled out accordingly.''

"But—where do I come into it?"

"Oh. Well, you were the man who got Ben Barstow hung originally. And you testified against the others. So we all voted you a share of the reward.''

"How much?" Toby whispered.

"Five hundred dollars." Loggins smiled. "Call it a wedding present.''

"You've done it!" I shrieked, throwing myself at the startled man. "You saved it!"

He caught me as I threw my arms around him. He managed to keep us both upright as I clung to his neck, laughing and he flung Toby a startled look.

"What's she talking about? Saved what?"

"The farm," said Toby, grinning broadly. "You've saved the farm.''

"Oh. Well, I'm glad of that." He smiled weakly as I

hugged him again. "I didn't know it was in trouble."

I disengaged myself from Loggins and went around the table to Toby. "We have to go now. I don't want to wait any longer."

"Go where?"

"To the bank. To Higgins. To tell him the land ain't his."

"Isn't," said Toby, and grinned. "Let's go."

Chapter Sixteen

Loggins came along with us. I asked why, and he said he didn't really need a reason, but if I had to know, he wanted a drink.

Toby agreed with him, but said he'd wait until our business was finished. I grinned at that. Our business. Banker Higgins wouldn't know what hit him.

I couldn't ignore the twinge of nervousness in my belly as we neared Ridgely. Not only would we settle the trouble over the farm, but it would be the first time anyone knew I had been the one to hide the witness. Even Abner Barton didn't realize that.

Loggins pulled up in front of Mick's saloon. He smiled down at us. "You two go on about your business. I'll be here—if you need me. I don't reckon you will."

I looked at him expressionlessly. "I never needed you before. I won't now."

His mustache twitched. "I reckon not, at that. Toby, come on by for a drink when you're finished. The first one's on me."

"What about me?" I demanded. "Am I supposed to

wait patiently out here while you two drink up a storm?"

Loggins pulled at his mustache. "I doubt you'll do it patiently, but you'll do it." He grinned, green eyes bright. "You've picked yourself out a man, Lonnie-girl, you'd best accustom yourself to it. Every wife does."

I hackled up, prepared to do battle, but Toby placed a hand on my arm. "You're both right, but I don't want to argue about it now. Understood?"

Loggins grinned amiably and swung off his horse. I stared at Toby and saw the stubborn set of his jaw. I couldn't fight them both, so I fought neither. Elegantly, I thought, I brushed a stray hair from my eye.

"Very well, gentlemen, we will not argue. Toby is free to drink with whom he chooses. However—" I paused significantly, and was rewarded with two pairs of attentive eyes on me— "However," I continued, "I expect it would be right kind if you brought a bottle home. The bride would like to imbibe a little, too."

Toby whooped with laughter and Loggins guffawed loudly. I sat primly aboard the buckboard seat and waited for the hilarity to subside. Finally both men quieted and I smiled serenely at them both.

"Are we agreed?"

Loggins shook his head. "Should've know. Girl like you will likely drink us both under the table."

"Then remember it, next time you invite my almost-husband to a saloon."

Loggins waved a hand. "You'll get your bottle, Lonnie. Now get along, before I escort you both into

245

that bank."

Toby grinned and lifted the reins, clucking at the mare to move her out. After a moment he slid me a sideways glance.

"You don't mean it."

"Mean what?"

"About the bottle."

I looked at him levelly. "Of course I do. This is a partnership, Toby Markham. You're no better than me. And I'll bet you I *can* drink you both under the table." I considered it a moment. "Well, maybe not Loggins. I expect he's got many a drinking year on us. But you—well . . ." I grinned.

His brows slid up. "You talk as if you really mean it."

"I do."

"Lonnie—whisky?"

"My pa," I said carefully, "liked a dram or two. When he died, he left behind two bottles." I slid him a look. "I drank them."

"Both?"

"Both."

He halted the mare before the bank, staring at me. "Have I got myself a drunkard for a wife?"

"I'm not a drunkard!" I flared. "And I'm not your wife yet!"

"All right!" he said hastily. "All right. You've made your point. And anyway, I'm not a big one for liquor. Every now and then, sure, but it's not a habit. You'll not lose me to the bottle, Lonnie."

I smiled to myself, content. "Good."

He jumped down and turned to help me climb out of the buckboard. I stood on the boardwalk before the

246

bank, staring at the gilt painting on the windows. Finally I looked at Toby.

"Let's get her done."

"Shall I . . ." He trailed off as I glared at him.

"This is *my* business, Toby. You just hold onto that money Loggins gave you."

"*Our* business," he retorted, planting his feet on the boardwalk as I started past.

I glanced back and saw the look in his eyes. "Our business," I echoed, and took his arm as he held it out to me.

Mr. Polt showed us in to see Higgins, after establishing that Toby wished to see him about my farm. The man was polite enough to Toby, but said nothing to me. It bothered me not at all, and I went softly into the office with Toby.

Higgins was seated behind his desk as we came before him and Polt introduced Toby, explaining his business. Toby had purposely neglected to tell Polt the nature of our relationship, and as far as Higgins knew, he was simply interested in buying the place.

Toby let me sit in the wooden chair, standing behind me, smiling gently at the banker. Higgins gestured Polt out of the office and seated himself behind his big desk.

"The Ryan place. Yes, it's for sale. But I must ask you why you've brought Miss Ryan along. She and I hardly see eye to eye on this matter."

Toby raised an eyebrow. "Well, sir, she is still the rightful owner. I felt she should be here."

Higgins pulled at a heavy, gray sideburn, thinking it over. At last he folded his hands and set them on the desk, leaning forward to look more closely at Toby.

"She threatened to stall the takeover any way she could. Do I have reason to believe she has brought you here for that purpose?"

Toby smiled easily, using all the bright charm I knew he had in abundance. "Of course not. I'm a buyer. Do you care to sell?"

The banker looked uncomfortable, shifting his substantial bulk in the chair. He shot a dark look at me but I remained suitably silent and innocent-looking. But I'd never tried it before and wasn't sure it was working.

"Well," finally replied Higgins, "in all truth I must say the property isn't entirely available at this moment. Not until the end of this week."

"Oh?"

"There's a time element, you see." Higgins glanced at me again, seemed satisfied with my expression and continued. "I'm sure Miss Ryan must have told you she has until the end of the week." He brightened. "Unless she's willing to leave sooner."

"No," I said flatly.

Toby's hand on my shoulder squeezed, and I said nothing more. Higgins studied me, but remained complacent. Toby, moving forward, leaned over the desk. He spoke very softly.

"Then the land isn't available for sale yet, is it? It isn't legally yours to sell." He smiled. "Is it?"

"Well . . ."

Toby's voice cracked across the room. "It's still hers, isn't it? Lonnie's. Not yours."

"Now wait just a minute," Higgins sputtered.

"It's mine," I whispered. "The land's mine."

"Only if you pay the debt!" Higgins snarled, glaring at me. "Abner Barton said you couldn't."

"I couldn't," I agreed. "Before."

Higgins' mouth dropped open as Toby began counting out the money. Finally the banker dragged his eyes to mine.

"You *did* bring him here. You *did* stage this entire meeting. You little—"

"No," I said clearly, "I did not. Toby is going to be my husband. There's an end to it."

Toby tapped the pile of bills. "There's an end to it," he echoed. "Right here. Bring out the lien. Now."

"I can fight you," Higgins said. "I can take it to the judge. He'll rule in my favor."

My head came up. "Which judge?"

"Jacob Macklin. Why?"

Satisfaction curled throughout my body. "He hated Jordy, you know. Hated his son. He was glad to hear he finally hanged."

Higgins stared at me. "What has that to do with this matter?"

"Toby is the witness who testified against them all. The Barstows. He's the man who got them hanged." I smiled. "Do you really think Jacob Macklin will take my farm away from the wife of the man who got his hated son hanged—legally?"

The banker's fleshy face slowly darkened. His shrewd eyes narrowed as he stared me down, but I refused to let him beat me. I stared right back, and after a long moment he cleared his throat.

"Missy, are you telling me—"

"You heard me," I said, interrupting curtly. "Toby is the witness. Jacob Macklin, glad as he was to hear of his son's death, would likely prefer to reward the man responsible." I smiled slowly. "Don't you think?"

"The deed," Toby said quietly.

Higgins' face whitened, then flushed dull red. For a moment I thought he might choke, but he had control of himself. Slowly he reached into his desk and brought out a folded paper which crackled as he flattened it out. He stared at Toby.

"You're only a boy. What do you know of business?" he said harshly, large hands spread across the deed.

My hackles came up, but Toby's hand dropped to my shoulder again and rested there. The calmness in his voice amazed me.

"Maybe—to some—I am just a boy. I'm not one to brag much, nor is it a thing I consider worthy of it, but keep in mind Kansas is rid of the Barstows. Your bank—your *town*—is a safer place without them." His fingers tightened on my shoulder. "Boy or not, Higgins, it's enough. Now, let Lonnie sign the deed."

Silently, heavily, the banker shoved a pen and bottle of ink across the desk at me. I picked it up and stared at the deed, seeing my father's signature. I signed my own name below it, then passed it to Toby.

"Wait," Higgins began.

I stared at him. "He signs, too. He's going to be my husband. Part-owner. This time we want everything very legal." I bared my teeth at him in a humorless smile. "The bank will have no claim on what's mine,

Higgins, ever again."

Toby silently signed the deed; Higgins witnessed it with his own scrawled signature; and it was mine once again.

I grinned up at Toby.

Ours.

Chapter Seventeen

Toby swung me up and against him as we stepped outside the bank, secure in the knowledge the land was clear. He smacked me a profound kiss before I could sputter out a protest and grinned happily down at me.

"It's done! It's for certain!"

I straightened my mussed dress. "What is?" I asked sourly, hoping no one had witnessed his display. I'd never been one to care what others thought before, but hiding a man for weeks was a whole different matter.

Toby tugged my braid. "Now we have to get married. You just made me part-owner. Either we have to get married, or I'm nothing more than a fancy hired hand."

I pulled a frown. "We've made a bargain. I'll keep to it."

He stared at me. Don't look so—so—dismal, Lonnie."

I laughed at him. "Toby, all I mean is you'd better treat me right. Or I'll throw you off my land right onto your ear."

He said nothing as I headed toward the buckboard. I started to climb into it, but he grabbed my arm and pulled me back down. I stared at him, perplexed by his odd expression.

"Let's go get it done."

"Get what done?"

"Getting married. There's nothing left for us to do, except make it legal. The land is yours—ours—so let's celebrate." He smiled slowly. "Let's not wait."

I gaped at him in a very unladylike fashion. "Toby—I need time."

"Time for what? I'm not about to let you think it over again. You might change your mind, as women are prone to do."

I glared at him darkly. "You don't know a thing about women, Toby Markham."

He laughed and lifted his brows. "Don't I, now? How would you know? I may be hiding all sorts of deep, dark secrets about my lewd past."

"Every man is due his secrets," I said calmly. "And every woman."

He stared at me consideringly. "Lonnie, is there something you're not telling me? Something I should know?"

I smiled crookedly at him. "If you should know it, you'll find it out. That, I think, is supposed to be a part of a marriage."

"Speaking of . . ." He took my arm and escorted me down the boardwalk.

"Where are we going?"

"To roust Loggins out of the saloon."

"What *for?*"

"I want him to stand up for me. I owe him a lot." I

felt his sideways glance. "So do you."

"I owe Dan Michael Loggins nothing!"

"Lonnie." Toby halted, stopping me before the saloon. "You owe the man your farm."

My mouth opened to protest, but I remained silent. He was right. When it came down to it, Toby was the one who actually got the Barstows hanged, but it was Loggins who tracked and caught them in the face of all odds.

And Loggins who had voted Toby the money.

I nodded. "Then get him. I'd be proud to have him at our wedding."

He smiled. "Wait here. I'll fetch him."

"I'd rather come in."

Now I'd exasperated him. "Lonnie, there are things a woman shouldn't do. Walking into a saloon is one of them."

"Mick knows me. Most of the town knows me. Nothing would hurt me."

He sighed. "Probably not, but it isn't seemly. I'm not the one to say what you can and can't do, but I wish you'd stay out here. Please?"

"God forbid *I* should ever do anything unseemly!" I exclaimed, and laughed.

"Lonnie."

I shoved at him. "Go get Loggins. I'll wait. I reckon I can start changing the me I've always been with this small step."

Toby tugged my braid again. "Just don't change yourself too much."

"Go!" I pushed him, and he went.

I sat on the bench outside and drummed my heels against the boardwalk, waiting impatiently. It wasn't that I wanted Toby out immediately so we could get ourselves married, but I knew I was a spectacle where I was. I'd found I was much more aware of looks people sent me as they passed by. I couldn't shrug the stares away anymore.

Loggins came out trailing pipe smoke and whisky fumes. I stared at him, astounded the man could have had so much in so short a time. His green eyes glinted mockingly at me as he swept off his hat.

"So, I'm to have the honor of seeing a promising soul hitched to the likes of you."

"You're drunk!" I accused.

Loggins returned his hat to his head. "Hardly, Lonnie, hardly. I've barely had enough to whet my parched throat. I was only remarking on the attributes of the girl my friend has had the audacity to find himself in love with."

I was on my feet, blazing at him. "I'm just as good as anybody else! You can't say I won't be a good wife to him! What do you know about me, anyway?"

He smiled sadly. "Probably more than you know. Like I said, you remind me of Charlotte. In some ways."

"Charlotte," I echoed, sobering. "I remind you of the wife that left you for another man?"

"Lonnie, Charlotte was Charlotte, and you are you." He dragged on his pipe. "I only meant you're just as determined to get what you want. In her case, she wanted someone else. In your case, you want Toby." He smiled beneath the mustache. "You're getting the better end of the deal."

Impulsively, I touched his arm. "Charlotte was a fool."

He grinned, eyes glinting, but I saw the sadness underneath. "Lonnie, my girl, that's enough to earn you your wedding gift. Here."

I stared blankly as he took something from beneath his coat. A bottle of whisky.

"Dan Michael," Toby began reprovingly.

We both ignored him, and I smiled slowly into the man's weathered face. Words were not needed, and I accepted his gift silently.

"Well," Loggins said brightly, "shall we find ourselves a preacher?"

"Wait!" I cried, flailing the bottle to hold them both back.

"Well?" Toby asked.

"There's—I . . ." I paused. "I have to do something. Make arrangements. Wear something."

"You look fine."

I stared at him. "This is an old dress I wore two years ago! It's too small, and it's all bleached out, and it's worn out. I can't wear it to my wedding!"

"You never cared before," Toby said lightly.

Loggins placed a firm hand on my shoulder. "You look fine. Like yourself. I never did think much of women who made themselves over into something they weren't just to get married. If a man don't know by then what he's getting, there's no sense in trying to disguise the issue."

"You," I began, but he smiled serenely at me and shoved me toward Toby.

"Will you take your woman in hand, my young friend, and explain matters to her? Otherwise she'll insist on wearing the trousers in this family."

Toby laughed. "Lonnie can wear what she likes. I

foresee no problems."

"Why don't you two get married," I said between my teeth. "You seem to agree on matters so well."

"Maybe," Loggins drawled, "we should have her drink the whisky *before* the ceremony. Kind of soften her tongue a mite."

I glared at him and pointed down the street toward the little white church. "The preacher is there. You go tell him. Toby and I have something to do, first."

"We do?" Toby asked.

I handed the bottle back to Loggins. "We're going to meet some people. Keep my whisky for later."

Loggins raised his brows. "I can't go see a preacher about a wedding with liquor in my hands."

"Let alone on your breath," I jeered.

Loggins handed the bottle to Toby. "You take it. I'll see you in church."

The man walked off before I could protest, and Toby steered me down the boardwalk.

"Who do you want to see?" he asked. "And why?"

"We must see Abner Barton. I want him to give me away."

"Who?"

I smiled crookedly. "He's my second father. Like Loggins is yours."

That drove Toby into silence, and we arrived at the smithy without further conversation.

Barton was deep in fitting a shoe to an old piebald gelding as we came on him at the smithy. He had the left hind leg hooked on his knees between his legs, nails in his mouth, judging how much more shaping he needed to do. He glanced up and nodded at me.

"Almost done."

I smiled and swallowed as his eyes slid over Toby, but Barton paid no more attention to us. The shoe was a proper fit so he took a nail and inserted it into one of the shoe slots, then tapped it with the hammer. Certain it was properly placed, he drove the nail in rapidly and finished off the others as quickly.

Toby waved away a fly and I seated myself on the large tree stump by the doors. Barton clipped off the protruding nail tips, then clinched them down. He had the rasping left to do, but decided it could wait. He dropped the hoof and stepped away from the gelding, smoothing out his leather apron.

"Lonnie, I'd planned on coming by your place later. You've saved me a trip."

I nodded as his eyes flicked to Toby. My almost-husband smiled a little, ill at ease from Barton's scrutiny, and I saw his face stiffen as Barton stared at the whisky bottle. I nearly laughed as Toby's whole body went still.

Barton snorted a little, dismissing Toby's innocent looks after a hard stare at the whisky. "You came in with Lonnie?"

"Yes, sir."

"She pick you up on the road?"

"No, sir."

"Then she must've found you at the saloon."

Toby swallowed. "No, sir, not the saloon. At the farm."

Barton's eyes hardened. "What were you doing there?"

Toby sighed and thrust the bottle at me. He faced

Barton squarely, and I wasn't certain who was the stronger man. Both of them were stubborn, I knew.

"Look, you must understand. Lonnie's been looking after me for some time. I was hurt, and she tended to me until I healed."

"*Lonnie* did?"

"Yes, sir. Last month."

"She said nothing to me about it."

I stood up, tucking the bottle into my folded arms. "I couldn't. Not a word. I couldn't tell a soul he was there."

"For lord's sake, Lonnie, why not?" Barton asked, staring at me in anguish.

"It isn't what you think," I said clearly. "He was hurt, and he had to be hidden."

"Hidden?"

"I was running," Toby said flatly. "Running scared from a group of men who wanted to kill me. They nearly succeeded, but Lonnie took me in until I healed. For her own safety, she could tell no one."

Knowledge crept into the blacksmith's eyes as he stared first at Toby, then at me. His voice came out hollowly.

"Lonnie—not the Barstows."

"The Barstows," Toby affirmed quietly. "I know what they did to Lonnie, sir; I know what you think of me for placing her in that position."

"He's the witness," I told Barton. "Toby's the one they wanted. I couldn't let him go, not when I knew they'd kill him. And I could tell no one."

Barton abruptly threw down the rasp he held and it clanged against the anvil. "You could have gotten her killed," he told Toby harshly.

259

"I know that, sir. Don't think I haven't cursed myself for it."

"For you she risked her life."

"Yes, sir. I know that."

Barton raised a threatening fist. "By rights I should take my fist to you for what you've done."

"I wouldn't blame you."

Toby, I realized, understood Barton's anger. But I didn't. "What are you doing? What do you mean?"

"This is something only he and I understand," Toby said quietly, meeting Barton's eyes. The blacksmith smiled briefly, acknowledging Toby's admission.

I glared at them both. "But *I'm* the one you're talking about. *I'm* the one in the middle."

"Lonnie," Barton began.

"No!" I cried. "You can't blame Toby, I won't have it! What I did, I did on my own. Because I wanted to. And Toby *wanted* to stay and fight when the Barstows came, but I sent him away. *I* did. He didn't run. He didn't leave me to those men. Don't you dare blame him for this!"

Barton, beginning to smile sadly, dropped his fist to his side. He shook his head and sighed.

"I guess it's come. I thought it might, one day. Well, there's only one reason you'd risk your life in quite this fashion for a man with a winning smile."

"I don't understand," I began, but Barton ignored me and looked steadily at Toby.

"Do you love her?"

"Yes."

He glanced at me. "I won't ask you. It shows in your eyes."

"Don't blame him," I said. "Don't hate him. Not you."

Barton engulfed my shoulder with a huge hand. "I don't hate him. I couldn't, not if you've settled on him. If he's the man you say he is, he's decent enough."

I smiled over at Toby. "He needs improving, but he'll learn."

Barton reached out to shake Toby's hand. "I won't hear of her being unhappy, will I?"

"Not if I can help it, sir."

"You don't have to call me *sir*." Barton shook his head. "I'm not Lonnie's father."

I reached up and hugged him, hard. "Maybe not," I said into his neck, "but you're the next best thing."

He untangled me, flushing, and cleared his throat. "Lonnie, I have to ask."

I was suddenly apprehensive. "Ask what?"

"The bottle. Why are you two toting around a bottle of whisky?"

"This?" I hefted it, grinning. "This is a wedding present. From someone you'll meet soon, if you'll come along to the wedding."

"Wedding." He nodded. "When?"

"Now," Toby said, dragging me next to him. "If I can ever get her to the church."

"You must give me away," I pleaded. "You must walk me down the aisle."

He spread his grimy hands, staring at them. "I'm filthy. I can't go like this. And there's Emily—"

"Go get her, and the boys." I grinned. "If I can get married looking like this, I'm happy enough to have you as you really are. We'll meet you at the church."

261

I tugged at Toby's arm. "We have to go tell Tolleson and the Swede. Toby, come on. Don't take root now."

We left Barton staring after us in shock, and I grinned happily. There was more fun to getting married than I'd thought.

Chapter Eighteen

The preacher stared hard at me when Toby finally got me inside the church. It had been years since I'd stepped inside it, for I'd found it difficult to return after attending the funeral of my family, and now I felt odd. I straightened my shoulders and pasted a weak smile on my face.

"Lonnie Ryan," said the old man, forcing a genuine smile past the reproach in his eyes. "Lonnie Ryan, you've come back into the fold and you're bringing a husband."

I slid a glance at Toby. "Well," I said uncertainly, "I am getting married. The 'fold' might come a little later."

The preacher nodded, taking my callused hand in his. "Whatever your reasons, I'm glad to see you again. I must admit I was surprised when this stranger came bearing such an odd tale."

Loggins, perched uncomfortably on the end of a hard pew, rose, hat in hands. He came forward and quirked a sandy eyebrow at me.

"I thought maybe you'd back out."

I glared at him. "I never back out of an agreement."

He nodded, fiddled with the hat, and sighed. His eyes slid around the interior and I realized he was highly discomfited. It amused me, and the smile I couldn't hide brought color to his dark face. His mustache twitched and he shook his head slightly.

"Lonnie, you're too perceptive for the likes of me."

"Don't matter," I retorted. "It ain't you I'm marrying."

"Isn't," corrected Toby, and took my hand from the preacher's into his own.

I shot him a disgusted look and then smiled weakly at the preacher. "Abner Barton and his wife and boys will be here soon. And Olaf Larsson, and Elmer Tolleson. It shouldn't be long. I'm sorry if we've interrupted."

The preacher's smile lit his face. "You're interrupting nothing, Lonnie! I'm glad to do this for you." His eyes slid uncertainly to Toby. "Even if I don't know the young man."

I jerked my hand from Toby's, startled by the realization of how our intimacy must look to the preacher, and did the introductions. Things eased a little then.

The Bartons came then, and the Swede joined us. Elmer Tolleson arrived on Larsson's heels. I swallowed and looked at Toby. He was a little pale, but his smile was the same.

"Let's get her done," Loggins announced.

The men, who had not the faintest notion who this man was, frowned at him. Once more I had to make the introductions, and once it was known Loggins had done the capturing of the Barstows, his presence was accepted with welcome.

Emily Barton pulled me aside and pressed a tiny bouquet of prairie flowers and blooms from her garden into my hand.

"Lonnie, I wish I'd known. We could have made a dress for you."

I glanced down at my faded yellow dress and nodded a little, knowing how I looked. But Toby had said he liked me this way, and I wasn't about to change on the spot. He'd have to take me the way I was.

"I guess I'll do," I said in a low voice.

She squeezed my shoulders. "You'll do fine. The kind of person you are has nothing to do with the way you look. All of us realize that." She looked across at Toby, saying something to her husband. "He sees it, at any rate. That's what counts."

I sighed heavily, suddenly afraid. "I reckon. Thanks for the flowers."

"Let's get her done," Loggins repeated, clearly uncomfortable.

I shot him a frowning scowl. "What's your hurry?"

He fingered his hat, still in his hands out of respect for the church. "I have to leave tomorrow morning. I'd as soon get you two married off so we can celebrate it before I have to go."

"Where are you going?" Toby asked sharply.

Loggins pulled at his mustache. "Got a job."

"Bounty hunting?" I asked disparagingly.

He flushed. "No. After the trial I got offered a job. Being sheriff in a little town south of here." He shrugged. "I got nothing better to do, and bounty hunting ain't entirely respectable. It'll do."

"*Isn't* respectable," I corrected, and felt unaccountably happy as I saw Toby's delighted grin. I nodded. "Let's get her done."

My guests took their places in the pews, and I grasped Abner Barton's strong arm. Toby sent me a long, eloquent look, then headed up the aisle to wait for my arrival.

It was a simple ceremony. We had neither organist nor many words to exchange, and I guess it was a pretty bare affair. But my friends watched, and it was all I cared about.

Toby, clutching my hand, went abruptly stiff when the preacher asked for a ring. I looked at him.

"Ring," he whispered, stricken. "I—I didn't think." He gazed at me. "Lonnie, I'm sorry."

"It don't matter," I said back. "A ring don't make a marriage."

"But . . ."

The preacher shook his head. "Young man, out here it isn't often a man can provide a ring. She's perfectly right in what she says. In the eyes of God you're married regardless of the ring."

I smelled whisky and tobacco as Loggins moved up behind Toby. He fumbled in a pocket. "I got one."

"A *ring?*" I asked. "You?"

He avoided my eyes and held something out to Toby. "Here, you have it. I got no use for it."

"Loggins," I began.

He shrugged. "It was Charlotte's. She left it behind, and I just sort of hung onto it. Perfectly good ring."

266

I stared at him, stricken, and after a moment Toby nodded silently. Loggins grinned lopsidedly and returned to his place. After a moment Toby slid the narrow gold band on my finger, and it was done. Except for the kissing part. That we got done too, though I flushed bright red before those watching. And then I was a wife.

We were hardly out of the church when Loggins cracked the bottle he had gifted me with. The preacher, who had come along to give us good wishes, glared at him disapprovingly, then vanished into his church. Emily Barton shook her head, then sighed. She smiled at me.

"Men and their whisky. Rarely do you get one without the other."

I laughed, then quieted as Loggins thrust the bottle at me. "Here," he said. "You be first. You're the bride." His eyes gleamed wickedly. "Besides, you claim you have a taste for it."

I grabbed it. "So I do," I told him, and proceeded to suck down a substantial swallow.

Silence greeted me when I handed the bottle back. Tolleson, Larsson and Emily Barton were shocked, but Abner Barton only smiled faintly and nodded. He knew me.

Loggins accepted the bottle. "One of these days, my girl, I'll discover something you can't do."

I laughed at him. "One of these days, sheriff, you'll realize there's *nothing* I can't do—if I feel like it."

Loggins prodded Toby's shoulder with a stiff finger. "Talk to the girl, laddie, or you'll be henpecked in no time at all."

Toby grinned companionably and captured the bottle, downing a deep swallow. Then he handed it across to Barton.

"Here, sir. I'd be pleased to have you drink with me."

Barton studied him seriously a moment, and I realized he was not entirely reconciled to him. Things had moved too fast for the blacksmith, and I knew I should have trusted him with the truth. I had hurt him.

The burly blacksmith lifted the bottle high. "This is no proper toast, since we have no readied glasses, but it'll serve." He smiled. "Here's wishing the best for them, and may their farm prosper."

"You know?" I asked, before he could drink. "You know it's clear?"

"Toby told me, Lonnie. He told me about the reward money Loggins brought him. That, more than anything, assures me he means only the best for you."

Loggins, who had slapped his hat back on, cleared his throat. "I must leave. I wish you all the best as well. Toby, take care of her." He grinned crookedly at me. "Maybe I should tell you to take care of him."

"You said you'd stay till morning!" I exclaimed.

"I'll start now. There's nothing for me here."

He moved past the others, heading for his horse. I left them all and trailed him into the street. He cinched his saddle tighter and untied his horse, peering around at me as I stood barefoot in the dust.

"You want something?"

"No."

He frowned at me, puzzled, then mounted with the enviable ease of a longtime horseman. From atop the dun he looked down upon me.

I patted the horse on the shoulder. "I wish you'd stay here."

His face was very still, but his eyes were bright. "I'll be around."

I said nothing until he lifted the reins and began to turn his horse. Then I put a hand out. "Loggins!"

He glanced down at me. "What is it?"

"Thank you. For everything. I—I . . ."

He understood as I trailed off. A bright smile stole across his face as he nodded. "I was wrong. You're nothing like Charlotte. Remember that, my girl."

"I will."

I watched until he was gone, and felt Toby's arm slide around my shoulders.

"He has to go, Lonnie. There are things he must do."

"He could do them here. Ridgely needs a sheriff."

"But Loggins needs something more than Ridgely."

I met his steady eyes. "Then you feel it too. The loneliness in his soul."

"Of course I do. But it's for him to diminish. Just as you had to diminish your own."

"I had help," I reminded him. "There's you."

He tugged my braid. "Just so you remember it."

"Something tells me you won't let me forget."

"Something tells me you're right."

I stared down at the ring shining on my hand.

Carefully I wiped a smear from it, then swallowed and looked at Toby, feeling odd. But happy.

"Ain't it pretty?" I asked softly.

He opened his mouth and our grins flashed at the same time.

"Isn't," we said as one.

THE NEWEST ADVENTURES AND ESCAPADES OF BOLT
by Cort Martin

#11: THE LAST BORDELLO   (1224, $2.25)

A working girl in Angel's camp doesn't stand a chance—unless Jared Bolt takes up arms to bring a little peace to the town . . . and discovers that the trouble is caused by a woman who used to do the same!

#12: THE HANGTOWN HARLOTS   (1274, $2.25)

When the miners come to town, the local girls are used to having wild parties, but events are turning ugly . . . and murderous. Jared Bolt knows the trade of tricking better than anyone, though, and is always the first to come to a lady in need . . .

#13: MONTANA MISTRESS   (1316, $2.25)

Roland Cameron owns the local bank, the sheriff, and the town—and he thinks he owns the sensuous saloon singer, Charity, as well. But the moment Bolt and Charity eye each other there's fire—especially gunfire!

#14: VIRGINIA CITY VIRGIN   (1360, $2.25)

When Katie's bawdy house holds a high stakes raffle, Bolt figures to take a chance. It's winner take all—and the prize is a budding nineteen year old virgin! But there's a passle of gun-toting folks who'd rather see Bolt in a coffin than in the virgin's bed!

#15: BORDELLO BACKSHOOTER   (1411, $2.25)

Nobody has ever seen the face of curvaceous Cherry Bonner, the mysterious madam of the bawdiest bordello in Cheyenne. When Bolt keeps a pimp with big ideas and a terrible temper from having his way with Cherry, gunfire flares and a gambling man would bet on murder: Bolt's!

#16: HARDCASE HUSSY   (1513, $2.25)

Traveling to set up his next bordello, Bolt is surrounded by six prime ladies of the evening. But just as Bolt is about to explore this lovely terrain, their stagecoach is ambushed by the murdering Beeler gang, bucking to be in Bolt's position!

WHITE SQUAW
Zebra's Adult Western Series
by E.J. Hunter

#1: SIOUX WILDFIRE   (1205, $2.50)

#2: BOOMTOWN BUST   (1286, $2.50)

#3: VIRGIN TERRITORY   (1314, $2.50)

#4: HOT TEXAS TAIL   (1359, $2.50)

#5: BUCKSKIN BOMBSHELL   (1410, $2.50)

#6: DAKOTA SQUEEZE   (1479, $2.50)

#7: ABILENE TIGHT SPOT   (1562, $2.50)

#8: HORN OF PLENTY   (1649, $2.50)

#9: TWIN PEAKS – OR BUST   (1746, $2.50)

Available wherever paperbacks are sold, or order direct from the Publisher. Send cover price plus 50¢ per copy for mailing and handling to Zebra Books, Dept. 1775, 475 Park Avenue South, New York, N.Y. 10016. DO NOT SEND CASH.